A Candlelight Ecstasy Romance ®

"YOU'RE RIGHT, KEEPING MY HANDS OFF YOU HAS BEEN A STRAIN. AND I'M NOT BIG ON MAKING LIFE ROUGH ON MYSELF."

Jason's eyes seemed to dilate, an engulfing darkness blotting out their blue hue, and she felt her heart quicken in dizzy reaction. And then he was pressing her gently down into the cushions, his arms around her waist and shoulders, his mouth searching relentlessly for hers.

Almost faint from excitement, Rachel was totally unable to think, and her lips opened helplessly under his. Some part of her knew she ought to protest, attempt somehow to push him away. But those warnings were lost in the overwhelming flood of other sensations claiming her. She moaned with half pleasure, half protest, as she felt the thrust of Jason's tongue probing the moist recesses of her mouth. A weakness seemed to invade her, as though her bones were melting, taking all her willpower with them.

A CANDLELIGHT ECSTASY ROMANCE ®

IN THE ARMS OF LOVE

Alexis Hill

A CANDLELIGHT ECSTASY ROMANCE ®

Published by
Dell Publishing Co., Inc.
1 Dag Hammarskjold Plaza
New York, New York 10017

To Linda, for everything.

Dell ® TM 681510, Dell Publishing Co., Inc.
Candlelight Ecstasy Romance®, 1,203,540, is a registered
trademark of Dell Publishing Co., Inc., New York, New
York.
ISBN: 0–440–14203–2

Printed in the United States of America
First printing—February 1983

To Our Readers:

We have been delighted with your enthusiastic response to Candlelight Ecstasy Romances®, and we thank you for the interest you have shown in this exciting series.

In the upcoming months we will continue to present the distinctive sensuous love stories you have come to expect only from Ecstasy. We look forward to bringing you many more books from your favorite authors and also the very finest work from new authors of contemporary romantic fiction.

As always, we are striving to present the unique, absorbing love stories that you enjoy most—books that are more than ordinary romance.

Your suggestions and comments are always welcome. Please write to us at the address below.

Sincerely,

The Editors
Candlelight Romances
1 Dag Hammarskjold Plaza
New York, New York 10017

CHAPTER ONE

Where did the summer go? Rachel Pritchard mused, smoothing a strand of dark red hair into the neat coil at the base of her slender neck.

Her gray eyes looked dreamily out the window of her second-floor office. On the campus walk below she could see a group of girls, obviously freshmen, exchanging jokes as they hurried toward the red-brick liberal arts building of Quincy Adams University. Were any of them in her English classes? the young woman wondered. And would one turn out to be that rare promising writer who would make the hard work of teaching Freshman Composition worthwhile?

The click of heels on the tile floor interrupted her musings. Rachel glanced up with a wide smile of welcome.

It was her colleague Marta Engle. At first glance the two young instructors seemed to have very little in common. But from the moment they'd met, Rachel had been delighted by Marta's whimsical sense of humor, and

Marta had liked Rachel's gentleness and sensitivity. They had become fast friends during Rachel's first year of teaching in Washington, D.C.

Marta looked rushed and slightly overweight in a black tentlike creation. As usual, tortoiseshell glasses sat askew on her straight nose, and nervous darts of limp brown hair framed her broad forehead.

"Well, back to the old grind," Marta sang out cheerfully, coming into the office and peering over Rachel's shoulder at the class lists on her desk.

Rachel had returned the friendly greeting and was just going to ask about Marta's weekend, when the young woman cut her short with a whistling, indrawn breath.

"My God, you've got him!" she crowed unexpectedly, pointing at one of Rachel's lists and squeezing her shoulder. "What luck! How'd you do it?"

Rachel stared at her friend blankly. What was she talking about? "Got whom?" she asked.

"Jason Brand. He's on your ten o'clock class list. The dirty dog has enrolled in Freshman Composition. Oh, what a joke!" Rachel stared curiously down at the printout. The name was there, close to the top. It was vaguely familiar, she thought, but it didn't ring any bells. Was he some notoriously difficult student whom she hadn't heard about? She fervently hoped not. Teaching was hard enough without a class troublemaker. Her eyebrows arched, and her gray eyes narrowed inquisitively.

"What in the world are you talking about, Marta? Who is Jason Brand?"

"Who is Jason Brand?" Marta repeated, looking astonished at Rachel's ignorance. "You mean, you really don't recognize the name? I know you specialized in the Victori-

8

an period, but don't you keep up at all with the current best-seller scene?"

And then the light dawned. The name was familiar because Rachel had read it in *The Washington Post* and *The New York Times* book reviews she studied weekly. Jason Brand was the reigning king of the nonfiction bestseller lists. A kind of modern muckraker with a fast-paced, colorful prose style, he had made himself famous with a series of books delving into various facets of American culture. His first success had been an explosive and bitterly funny book exploring the inner workings of the American Special Forces in Vietnam. He had followed that with an equally popular exposé of the fashion industry and an even more widely discussed book on the bizarre world of daytime-television game shows.

But she had never read any of his works. The subjects simply didn't interest her.

"Surely you can't mean that the Jason Brand on my class list is that—"

"The same," Marta interjected triumphantly. "I don't know the whole story. I just heard about it myself yesterday at the faculty tea you missed. But the word is that he's here doing research for his next best seller—something on undergraduate life in a typical American minor-league university. Maybe he chose us because his father lives in the area. Or maybe he's thinking about Congress as his next target and wants to start soaking up some of the local atmosphere."

Rachel's brows knitted in perplexity. "But how can he be enrolled in Freshman Comp?" she wondered aloud. "Surely he's already got a college degree."

"No. That's just the beauty of it," Marta countered, obviously richly amused. "He doesn't. Apparently he dropped out of high school and became a literary golden boy without any degree at all, thank you. And what's more, he's the most gorgeous thing you've ever set eyes on in your life! I caught a glimpse of him in the cafeteria—an Adonis in tight jeans and a black turtleneck. The female students were swooning at his feet like pigeons in heat. Do pigeons go into heat?" she asked as an afterthought, lifting a dark eyebrow. "Oh, well, that's certainly what they looked like." Still chuckling, Marta turned to leave.

But, though Rachel often laughed appreciatively at Marta's outrageous way of putting things, this time she was not amused. She was beginning to remember enough of the author's reputation to know that he delighted in scrutinizing his subjects with the relentless curiosity of a scientist peering through an electron microscope. And it seemed likely he had signed up for Freshman Composition looking for something to ridicule. Marta might view the whole thing as a joke, but she was inclined to see Jason Brand as a threat.

What had Charles Riddle meant by assigning Brand to her? A dark suspicion began to form at the back of her mind. Riddle, the chairman of the English department, was recently divorced. Once liberated, he had started behaving like an uncaged satyr. He had spent the concluding months of the spring semester trying to persuade Rachel to go to bed with him. She had refused and he hadn't liked that. Riddle was known for a streak of sadistic humor. Was giving her the "honor" of teaching Brand a way of getting back at her? She wouldn't put it past him. Maybe he was looking for an excuse to dismiss her and hoped Brand would supply one. Rachel sighed. Just when she was beginning to feel she'd made a place for herself, Fate seemed to be having its way with her again.

I'm going to have to be very careful this semester, she warned herself as she gathered up her books and papers.

On the way down to her first class she made a brief stop at the women's room. She was always careful to check her appearance before facing a group of students. A wry twist of amusement quirked her lips. The first day of class they would be watching with critical eyes, hoping for some reason not to take her seriously. An undone button or zipper, a bit of slip showing beneath a hem, and the whole semester might go wrong. But she was too good a teacher to let her students get sidetracked in that way.

Eyeing her reflection, she touched her auburn hair and checked the waistband of her straight khaki skirt. Her tailored white blouse was firmly tucked in. Nothing was showing that shouldn't. Her inspection, though thorough, was routine—unlike two years ago when, as a graduate student at Winthrop University in Boston, she had stared eagerly at the mirror, making every effort to look her best before heading off for Jonathan Convers's Victorian poetry seminar. Then the charcoal liner edging her gray eyes was meticulously applied, there was just the right hint of blusher on her high cheekbones, and her dark red hair was coaxed into a seemingly artless cascade spilling over her shoulders. Now, beyond appearing neat and presentable, she really didn't care much about her looks.

She paused, eyeing the rather buttoned-up image in the mirror pensively. Maybe it was time to start caring again. In fact, maybe it was high time. Was she going to allow something that had happened in Boston a year and a half ago to blight her life permanently?

Where's your spunk? Rachel asked herself, her mouth twisting in grim self-mockery as she started to recall the past.

11

But just then two giggling students pushed open the swinging door, and Rachel was brought forcibly back to the present. A quick glance at her watch told her she couldn't dawdle any longer, and she turned toward the door.

The moment she walked into her classroom she spotted Jason Brand from the corner of her eye. He stood out like a panther in a cage of tabby cats. Setting her papers and books on the metal table and turning to the blackboard, she quickly printed ENGLISH 0100 and MS. PRITCHARD in firm, round letters. Then she swung around to face the class.

At first glance the rest of the students appeared to comprise the usual mixture. They seemed scattered haphazardly around the room, eyeing her with varying measures of hopefulness, hostility, and apprehension. A thin girl with long brown hair was sitting to the left near the front, seesawing a ballpoint pen between her fingers. The poor girl is obviously nervous, Rachel thought. She gave the student an encouraging smile, then turned her head, surveying the room. Her smile became less encouraging as she spotted a pair of boys with wrinkled plaid shirts and hair spilling over their ears, whispering in the back. They looked like trouble. Was there some way of separating them? Should she make a seating chart? She'd resorted to the technique with other classes. But she wasn't going to give Jason Brand the opportunity to write about the way freshman English teachers treated college students like fifth-graders.

Brand was in the corner, two rows from the front. She forced her eyes to move quickly past his dark leonine

12

head. But his image had already etched itself in her mind's eye.

He was very much at ease, his long blue-jean clad legs stretched out in front of him and crossed indolently at the ankles. Though he was seated, it was obvious that he was a tall, powerfully built man. The way his expensively cut tweed jacket molded to his broad shoulders; the way the muscles of his thighs strained against the taut material of his jeans told her that. His blatant and superb masculinity made the angular adolescent youths around him look unfinished.

His presence was so overpowering that for a brief moment Rachel felt as though she were alone in the room with him. But she quickly shook off the notion.

What was wrong with her? Jason Brand might be what some women referred to as a "hunk," but that sort of man had never attracted her. In the past it was another type entirely who had made a fool of her, she admitted, blinking back the stab of pain that always came with that memory.

Forcing herself to concentrate on her lesson plan, she introduced herself and then began to read from the class list, asking first in a soft, professorial voice, "If I mispronounce your name, please correct me."

Jason Brand's name was the second to be read. When he replied—in deep tones edged very slightly with amusement—she glanced up and found her gray gaze locked with a pair of cobalt-blue eyes that were observing her with unnerving intensity through a half closed screen of dark lashes. Looking down quickly, she rushed on to the next name.

After going through the class list, Rachel spent half an hour laying down some ground rules, going over the semester's work, and answering questions. The first-day procedures always made her feel a little like a top sergeant, but she knew that she would be better friends with her students in the long run if she made all the rules clear at the beginning.

After the business part of the class was over, she turned her attention to something she always looked forward to—journals. Picking up her stack of mimeographed journal entries, she distributed them at the ends of the rows. This was one way her class differed slightly from others. As a young girl, Rachel had always kept a journal. It had been an outlet for all her private thoughts and tender imaginings, and it had helped develop her writing skill. She was convinced her students could also benefit from the habit.

"A journal is a sort of intellectual diary," she explained to the group. "It's an opportunity to write about your ideas and feelings and express thoughts more clearly. You are not required to keep a journal; but if you do, it will count favorably toward your final grade—depending, of course, on how much effort you've put into the project. And if any of you are thinking about trying for an A, you should definitely plan on keeping one."

She paused to glance around at the class. Many of the faces looked perplexed. It always took awhile for new students to catch on to the idea, she had found; but when they did, they often discovered they liked it.

"You can write in your notebooks about anything you wish," she continued warmly. "And the entries may be of any length. Unlike your other papers, journal entries will not be graded or corrected for spelling, punctuation, or grammar. I want you to feel relaxed about writing." She smiled. "To give you an idea of the sort of thing I mean,

14

I've handed out samples of what other people have done. I suggest you look them over.

"If you decide to keep a journal," she went on pleasantly, "I'll ask you to hand it in once every three weeks. Skip a line between entries, and leave one side of the page blank so I can comment if I want. Any questions?" Rachel looked around expectantly. The shy girl with the pen had her hand half raised.

"Yes, Ms. Sachs?" Rachel asked kindly.

"Will anyone but you see what we write?" The girl blushed with discomfort.

"No. I'm the only one, unless you give permission to show it. And that's a promise," Rachel added. Looking up, she noticed that Jason Brand was grinning. What was there to grin about? Surely he didn't intend to keep a journal. But of course not. There was no reason for him to go to so much trouble.

She dismissed the class and watched the students begin filing out. Several gathered around her desk to ask questions they'd been too shy to raise before. As she handled each student's problem, one by one they drifted away. But after the last girl had departed, the room still wasn't empty. Jason Brand hadn't left his seat. He was still lounging in the corner of the room. Beginning to pile up her books and papers, she gave him an inquiring look. But he simply uncoiled his long body, got to his feet, and moved toward her casually, favoring her with a slow smile. His intent blue eyes never wavered from her face; and, to her horror, she found herself blushing. Rattled by this sudden attack of postadolescent shyness, she had to force herself to meet his look steadily. Supremely confident men like him made her nervous, but she simply wouldn't allow herself to be cowed either by his reputation or his rather overwhelming physical presence.

"I thought they'd never leave," he drawled, his face lighting up with a warm intimacy that took her breath away. But Rachel had regained her self-control and, despite her recent self-questioning, the protective wall she had built around herself since graduate school was back in place.

"I beg your pardon?" she asked politely.

He moved closer so that his legs were near the edge of her desk, and she was forced to tip her head back to look up at him. It took determination to keep a serene expression on her face, because her heart was pounding. Why? she wondered. It had been a long time since her pulse had raced this way over the nearness of a man. The fact unnerved her.

"I thought I should say hello," he announced, shooting her an engaging smile that revealed a set of perfect white teeth.

Keeping her own polite expression carefully in place, Rachel replied evenly, "I already know who you are and why you're here."

His eyes were glinting appreciatively over her features as though he thought they were going to be lovers. And she felt the hairs on the back of her neck prickle.

"Yes, well, I'm here to do some research," he went on. Then he paused, seeming to expect some response. But she locked her jaws together and kept her gray eyes lifted in neutral inquiry. She was determined not to let him suspect the effect he was having on her.

"I was impressed by the way you conducted this first class," he said. "You've obviously had some experience dealing with college freshmen. I'd like to discuss it with you."

"You could interview me sometime during the office hours I've posted," she replied pleasantly.

He paused briefly. Then, putting his large long-fingered hands down flat on the desk top, he leaned over so that he was disturbingly close to her. Defensively she pushed her chair backwards.

"I was thinking of something less formal," he murmured, smiling into her guarded eyes. "I was wondering if I could discuss it with you over dinner sometime this week?"

Rachel blinked. She hadn't been prepared for anything quite so direct. For a moment she considered the idea. Maybe it was time for her to come out of the protective shell she had built around herself. Accepting a dinner invitation might be a good idea. But an invitation from Jason Brand? No, she told herself. Absolutely not. It was an invitation to play with dynamite.

"I'm very flattered," she said in a polite but distant tone. "but I'm afraid I must refuse. You are enrolled in my class; and even though you're not the usual type of student, still, I make it a point not to accept dates with anyone I'm teaching. I'm sure you can understand why. And now if you'll excuse me, I have another lecture this morning."

"I see." There was a brief moment of strained silence. Then he straightened and brushed his jacket back to slip his hands into his pockets. The action revealed a narrow waist and lean hips.

He gave Rachel an amused, assessing stare that she did her best to meet neutrally. "Very professional of you, and I do admire professionalism—though one can take it too far," he added, his firmly modeled lips twisting in a wry grimace. "Still, I regard myself as crushed but not defeated. Do you hold out any hope for the end of the semester?"

Despite herself Rachel felt her lips begin to lift in a half smile and hurriedly tightened them. He was much too charming and sure of himself.

"The end of the semester is a long way off," she told him primly. But she knew by his own grin that he had seen her weakening.

"Then I'll just have to count the days," he murmured, before turning slowly and sauntering out with lazy grace.

Rachel watched his exit with a small, inward sigh of mingled relief and regret, then quickly gathered up her books.

Some of Rachel's tension drained away after she went through the orientation with her next class. It was disturbing to realize just how much Jason Brand's presence earlier had affected her actions and emotions.

After answering another round of questions at the end of the session, Rachel made her way back upstairs. Through the open door to the outer office, she could hear the sound of voices. Marta and one of the new Freshman Composition instructors, Melissa Waddington, were chatting in the anteroom.

"Join us for lunch at the faculty dining hall," Marta suggested cheerfully. "We're going to celebrate the start of the yearly ordeal by splurging."

Rachel agreed readily. The Faculty Club, with its linen tablecloths, good food, and Williamsburg decor, was one of the benefits of teaching at Quincy Adams. And besides, she'd been looking forward to a companionable chat with Marta.

18

As she and the two other young women headed across the campus to the Faculty Club, she gave her new colleague a surreptitious inspection. Melissa was an expensively dressed honey blonde, with the polish of a debutante. Rachel wondered why she had taken a job as a freshman English instructor—certainly not for the salary.

In the dining room the threesome made their selections from the buffet line and paid the cashier. Then they found a pleasant table beside a sunny window and a screen of bushy ferns and graceful schleffleras.

"Well, have you decided which contemporary fiction to have your students read?" Rachel asked Melissa, trying to make the new faculty member feel at home. She could remember only too well how out of it she had felt on her own first day of classes at Quincy Adams. As she spoke she poured tangy dressing over the crisp green of her chef salad.

"I've been thinking about Vladimir Nabokov," Melissa replied. "If he's not too advanced for Freshman Comp, that is."

"*LOLITA?*" Marta shouted with an explosive crack of laughter, a forkful of beef stew stranded in midair between dish and mouth. "Why should they waste time reading about an old lecher when they can see our respected department chairman in action firsthand?"

"Shhhh." Rachel giggled, looking around with half serious apprehension. "Do you want to put all our heads on the chopping block?"

Marta snickered mischievously but lowered her voice and her fork. "You're right," she agreed wryly, her words pitched in an exaggerated stage whisper.

"What are you talking about?" Melissa questioned.

"Didn't Charles Riddle make a pass at you when you came in for an interview?" Marta prodded. "He does it to everyone, but a stunner like you would be more his type. How about it, Melissa?"

The young woman smiled knowingly, accepting the compliment as a matter of course. "Please call me Muffy; all my friends do," she replied in silken tones. "Yes, he did give me the eye when he talked about the job. But I know I can handle his type. And I am wearing an engagement ring," she said, flashing an enormous emerald-cut diamond.

Her fiancé must be rich, Rachel mused. That rock she's wearing probably cost the earth. But I'll bet it won't put Riddle off. In two weeks he'll undoubtedly be spouting that tired line at her—the one he gave me last year about how it will give you depth to learn the art of love from an experienced and sensitive teacher. *Should I warn her?* Rachel asked herself. Although Melissa had a brittle exterior that made her seem experienced, the hard facade might be a cover for vulnerability. Hadn't her own polished exterior once hidden an innocent? Her gray eyes clouding with concern, Rachel was about to caution the new instructor when Marta's voice interrupted her thoughts.

"Who cares about Charles Riddle. I'm more interested in hearing about Jason Brand. Stop holding out on us, Rachel. How was your ten o'clock class?"

Rachel shifted uneasily, feeling a shiver run up her spine. She had no desire to talk about the writer, but she could see it was going to be unavoidable. "Unnerving," she said. "You don't really think he would have signed up for Freshman Comp if he didn't plan to write something scathing about the experience for his latest painstakingly researched money-maker, do you?"

"Well, I'd like to have him," Muffy interjected. "And I don't mean just as a student. I bet he'd make a fantastic lover."

Rachel's eyes widened, and she struggled to repress a laugh at her own ingenuousness. Obviously Muffy was no innocent in need of warning.

Marta's eyebrows shot up. "But you're engaged!" she blurted out.

"Oh," Muffy said, making an airy, dismissive gesture. "Eliot and I have an agreement. He's doing an internship with International Energy in Paris this year. My parents insisted that I stay in the States, and Daddy got me this job to keep me out of trouble. But while the cat's away, the mice will play." She winked. "Eliot and I don't bother each other about it."

Is that how the other half lives? Rachel wondered, shocked in spite of herself. And, glancing up, she noted Marta's strained expression and knew that Muffy's revelation had been a bit too much for her friend too.

Marta cleared her throat. "Well, you've got to admit that it's pretty impressive that Jason Brand became a best-selling author without even going to college," she observed brightly, to change the subject.

"You're right about that," Rachel agreed, also glad to start on a new topic. "Getting published is so hard." All her life she'd been writing, but so far all she'd got out of it was disappointment. The novel she'd shoved in her desk drawer this summer was an excellent case in point.

"Do you write books?" Muffy queried, a spark of interest in her expertly made-up eyes.

"Uh, yes," Rachel mumbled, sorry they'd started on this topic after all.

"Have any of them been published?" Muffy pressed.

"No," Rachel admitted, aware that color was creeping up her neck. She didn't want to parade her raw feelings about her drawer full of rejection slips in front of Muffy.

Glancing up, Rachel saw that Marta was looking at her with sympathy. When she had been really low, she had confided to her friend her frustration and disappointment over having her manuscripts returned time after time. Marta understood how sensitive she was on the subject. But clearly Muffy didn't know—or didn't care.

"Well, what do you think Jason Brand has that you don't?" Muffy bore on relentlessly, a malicious gleam in her eyes. "How come he got his work published and you can't?"

The question was a blow below the belt. And Rachel responded like a wounded boxer. "I don't know," she flashed recklessly. "Maybe he went to bed with his editor. That's probably what it takes to get into print these days. And Jason Brand doesn't look like the type to have any scruples," she added sarcastically. "In fact, he looks like the sort of man who would stop at nothing to get his way." Even to her own ears she sounded as though she were overreacting. But she couldn't stop herself. It was a combination of her own frustration and her resentment over the way Jason Brand had unsettled her earlier, making her feel stirrings of awareness she had not experienced in a long time.

"Well, you *do* have to admit he's gorgeous," Muffy persisted with a toothy laugh. "How are you going to take comma splices seriously with something as sexy as that in

22

the room? I'd forget everything the minute he looked at me."

Rachel had had more than enough. Pushing her chair away from the table, she fumbled for her purse and stood up.

"I'm not attracted to shallow men like Mr. Brand," she snapped. "Those macho types don't appeal to me. I like some spark of sensitivity in a man's face. Jason Brand leaves me totally cold," she insisted—guiltily aware that the angry statement was a lie.

Excusing herself, she stepped around the cluster of potted plants screening the next table only to be knifed by a pair of icy blue eyes. They belonged to Jason Brand. He was sitting in a casual position, but the way his tanned fist curled around his china coffee cup suggested he was on the point of snapping off its white handle.

Oh, God, she thought with a sinking feeling; *He's heard every stupid word I just said. And I went to such lengths to be diplomatic this morning.* She cursed her unguarded tongue, for obviously she had now undone that diplomacy. The tight expression on his handsome features told her that. Flushing, she looked away and hurried toward the swinging doors leading upstairs.

CHAPTER TWO

Two days later Rachel approached her ten o'clock class with foreboding. Dozens of times she had started for the English department office to ask Charles Riddle to switch Jason Brand to a different class. But something had always stopped her. She told herself it would be too humiliating an interview with the department chairman. But in the back of her mind she wondered if that was her real reason. Maybe, she told herself, Jason Brand would take the initiative and request another instructor. He must realize now how impossible the situation was.

But when she pushed open the door to Room 57B, there he was, occupying the same seat, stretched out in the same indolent attitude of repose. She could feel his glance boring into her as she walked to her desk. Trying to ignore it, she put her books down and began the day's lesson. What must he think of her after that ridiculous outburst in the cafeteria? *I can just imagine,* she assured herself sardonically. *I thought I was going to be so cool and profes-*

24

sional. And already I've made a fine mess of things. The man is probably dreaming up ways to get even right now— and I can't really blame him, she acknowledged.

Yet, come what may, Rachel refused to allow the tension he created in her to affect her teaching.

Jason Brand never missed a day and was always there in the corner when she entered the room. Although he never made a move, never said a word, he watched her constantly. But then so did her other students; she was used to it.

In the second week she assigned a short essay asking students to narrow a broad topic and construct an introduction and conclusion. The efforts of the others, of course, looked pathetic next to the smooth professionalism of Jason Brand's essay. But while his polished and focused essay was obviously the work of a skilled writer, she would not have called it brilliant. And she knew now that he was capable of brilliance, for she had taken the trouble to read his book on Vietnam—a work that had disturbed her but had also forced her grudging admiration. In his essay, though, the writer had not gone to any special lengths to impress her. Oddly, this fact was reassuring. She wrote "A" and "Excellent" on the paper and handed it back with a bland smile. A few other students also got good grades; among them, surprisingly, was the shy Ms. Sachs.

During the third week, when journals were due, Rachel got her first hint of what was going on in Jason Brand's mind while he lounged so silently in the corner of the room.

At the end of class the half dozen students who had decided to keep journals deposited their hardcover notebooks on her desk. Jason Brand was the last to leave. As

25

he moved past her desk he paused to place a notebook on top of the pile. She glanced up at him, her eyes widening with astonishment.

"Surely you're not going to bother with a journal," she burst out. "You must know it's quite unnecessary."

"Oh, but I want to," he drawled in his deep voice, flashing a hard smile that did not reach his eyes. "I may be just a shallow, defenseless freshman, Ms. Pritchard; but where you're concerned, I aim to please."

Her mouth dropped open. What did he mean by that? With a surge of discomfort, she remembered the scene in the cafeteria. Had she actually been stupid enough to call him shallow? Should she apologize now? she asked herself. But before she could say anything more, he had turned to move out the door with the other students.

Rachel didn't get around to looking at the journals until that night. She began to go through them while she was eating dinner. They were the usual: poetic entries describing sunsets, amateurish psychological studies analyzing relationships, and accounts of sports triumphs. But some of the writers made her smile with pleasure, particularly Ms. Sachs, who really seemed to have sensitivity as well as the talent to put her feelings into words.

On all the journals Rachel was careful to write a number of encouraging comments to let their budding authors know she was interested in what they had to say. But with Ms. Sachs she went a bit further. "You have a sensitive style and a colorful touch with description. But you could do more with your imagery. If you'd like to come to my office, I'd enjoy talking with you about it," she wrote, smiling to herself. You had to be so careful with the ego of a young writer. She remembered how wounded she had been by criticism at that age. "And I'm not all that hard-boiled now," she muttered ruefully.

She put Jason Brand's journal off until last, opening it with a reluctant sigh. Why was he bothering? Really, it was ridiculous.

He wrote in black pen with thick, slanting strokes. It began:

> Journal-keeping has always struck me as a rather narcissistic occupation. However, I think gauging my psychic temperature for the benefit of Ms. Pritchard may turn out to be amusing.

Rachel put her forkful of salad down impatiently. He made it sound as if she were some sort of voyeur, when in actuality she had tried to discourage him from turning in a notebook. She couldn't care less about his "psychic temperature!"

It went on:

> There are several reasons why I decided to research a private college. I've never had a high opinion of the hallowed tradition of a college education for the masses. Though I didn't go to college myself, and in fact never officially graduated from high school, my father was a professor at Johns Hopkins—but not your typical dusty academic type. The old man and I didn't get along, and I suppose that may have something to do with my prejudices. He was a born lecturer. Too bad he had a son who hated being lectured.
>
> I could never stomach sitting around like an empty

box while some fool of a pedant entertained himself filling me up with his half-baked ideas.

No, Rachel thought, pausing to take a sip of coffee. Judging from his book, which described his stint in the Special Forces during the war, he was too full of his own ideas to accept anyone else's. He must have been impossible as a teenager; and growing up in the turbulent Sixties, of course, would have made it that much worse. She sympathized with his father.

Rachel concentrated on the stark slanted handwriting and began reading again.

However, I'm interested that most Americans romanticize the idea of a college education for their kids. Those who don't credit the public institutions with enough status set their caps for a second-rate private college like Quincy Adams, where the tuition is three times as high. I'm curious to see if they're getting anything for their money.

As I'm contemplating a book on the subject, I signed up for Freshman Composition so I could sample a required course here. And after just a few weeks of research I can already envision a chapter entitled "The Psychology of the Frustrated Female Freshman English Instructor."

Naturally I'd make my heroine lithe and nubile, with firm breasts, a narrow waist, and legs that belong on a Las Vegas runway. And since my tastes run to the exotic, I might even stretch the imagination and give her smoky gray eyes and dark red hair. I admit it's absurd to postulate such a luscious creature parading around in front of a bunch of adolescents and spouting nonsense about independent clauses and participial phrases. But like the old cliché, sometimes truth is stranger than fiction.

Rachel choked on her sandwich, coughing and sputtering while the crumbs lodged in her dry throat. Jumping to her feet, she rushed to the sink and took several swallows of water. My God, it was perfectly obvious that he was talking about her! Furious, she marched back and picked up the notebook as though it were a viper.

Since my chapter would analyze the psychology of this fascinating instructor, I'd have to give her a few quirks. The young woman I have in mind hides her promising red hair away in a bun. She wears outfits that could neutralize the hormones of a platoon of libidinous twenty-year-olds marooned with her on a desert island. A psychologist might call the old-maid ensembles a deliberate tease and speculate that she enjoys displaying herself in these guises.

And what about her own hormones? From the way our heroine packs her prim little blouses, she's definitely got more than her quota. And yet she's the type who goes around denying she finds grown men attractive. She may even be tasteless enough to do it in public places like the Faculty Club. Why all these disclaimers? Do they mask a fear that she's really not woman enough to handle an adult male?

There was more, but Rachel refused to read on.

The nerve of the man! Just what did he think gave him license to speculate about her like that? And just this morning, she fumed, she had been on the point of apologizing to him! Now she was delighted that she had missed the chance. Blazing with righteous indignation, she snapped the horrible notebook shut, took it to the stove, and held it over the gas flame until the pages began to blacken and curl. The thought of Jason Brand chuckling maliciously as he wrote sent the blood pounding to her temples. She could imagine how amused he must have been anticipating her reaction. And here she was, playing right into his hands. But she couldn't help herself.

Flinging the ruined journal into the garbage, Rachel began to pace the kitchen floor, clenching and unclenching her fists. Men, she thought. They all had one-track minds. Even with Jonathan, whom she had believed was different, it had ultimately come to that.

Sitting down at the kitchen table, she put her head in her hands. And then it all came flooding back, in a kaleidoscope of images: scenes from her last semester in graduate school in Boston. It had been a semester of heaven and hell for Rachel; because, before she knew how it happened, she had fallen in love for the first time—and with a man who was not free to return her affections.

Her advisor had suggested that she take the Victorian poetry seminar with Jonathan Convers. He was the prize new faculty member everyone was talking about at Winthrop University. And Rachel had been flattered by the recommendation, but also a little nervous that she wouldn't measure up.

She needn't have worried. Professor Convers had given her first paper—entitled "Victorian Morality in the Poetry of Elizabeth Barrett Browning"—an A. Later he had asked her up to his office for a friendly argument over some of her conclusions. And she had gone eagerly, despite her roommate's raised eyebrows. She knew some professors liked to flirt with their students, but she was convinced that Jonathan's interest in her was purely intellectual.

She had defended her paper well. And Professor Convers had been impressed, his dark eyes sparkling on her face as he listened. It was exciting to have a man of his intellectual ability interested in her opinions, and their meeting turned out to be the first of many discussions in which Rachel found herself talking more and more freely about her aspirations and dreams. She even brought Professor Convers some of the short stories she was writing. And he had encouraged her to send them to well-known literary magazines. When they came back with printed rejections, he had not let her give in to discouragement.

"You have real ability," he told her, a smile touching his shapely mouth. "And I expect to see your name in print someday."

He was a slightly built man, only an inch or two taller than Rachel herself, with thick pale hair that framed an intense, sensitive face. But it was his quick mind that made her think of him as special.

As a beautiful girl, she had been pursued by many of the young men who were her fellow students. And she had enjoyed the attention; had enjoyed her share of casual student romances. But during her undergraduate years she had preferred not to become seriously emotionally involved with anyone. And after she met Jonathan, she was glad, because the young men who were her fellow students suddenly seemed shallow. She couldn't take them seriously anymore except as friends. Jonathan Convers was so different. She was bowled over by his wit and charmed by the fact that such an impressive scholar seemed to be taking her opinions seriously.

It was about that time that the Bedford Poetry Society gave him a substantial grant to write a book called *The Sensibilities of the Victorian Poets.* He asked Rachel to be his research assistant; she accepted without hesitation, ignoring warnings from several graduate students who had slyly suggested that his interest in her might not be entirely academic. But by that time she had put him on a pedestal and had absolute faith in his integrity. Besides, he was married; and she had never thought of herself as the home-wrecking type.

When he asked her to call him by his first name, "to make their working relationship smoother," she had believed he meant exactly what he said and nothing more. Looking back, she now saw herself as incredibly gullible.

At first she and Jonathan had made a good team, digging shades of meaning out of the works of Tennyson, Matthew Arnold, the Brownings, and the Rossettis. Rachel found herself rushing through her own course work so she could spend more time researching background material for Jonathan. Her notes were careful and precise, and her spirits soared from his praise.

But at the same time, she began to sense a tension in the room when they were alone together. When she sat next to him on the office sofa, sometimes she felt he was too close. Often she would have to get up to clear her head. And she began to suspect from the warm tones of his usually authoritative voice and the caressing looks he cast her that his interest might not be purely academic after all.

Sometimes his hand touched hers as he gave her an index card, and she trembled at the contact. He seemed to be able to make strong flutters of sensation shiver through

32

her body, as though the temperature in the room were somehow out of kilter. But she told herself that there was bound to be some sexual tension between any man and woman working so closely together. Because she didn't want to give up the relationship, she ignored the warning signals.

Nevertheless, one fine spring afternoon as she sat in the campus library staring out the window at the delicate green of the budding leaves, she couldn't deceive herself any longer. She was falling in love with Jonathan Convers. The feeling had been building for some time. And once she inwardly admitted that fact, she knew she could no longer go on working for him. Sooner or later they would end up in bed together, and she wasn't prepared to deal with the relationship on that level.

The next afternoon Rachel sat beside Jonathan on the office couch, steeling herself to resign as his assistant. Unexpectedly he leaned over her to retrieve a pencil, and his fingers brushed against the front of her blouse. It was as if a spark of electricity had leaped from his fingers to her body. He must have felt it too.

"Oh, Rachel," Jonathan groaned. And then he folded her into his arms, his lips swooping to take possession of hers.

At first she was stiff with shock, paralyzed by the overpowering sensations flooding her. But as Jonathan pushed her back against the sofa she felt herself responding to his ardor.

Though Rachel had admitted to herself that she loved Jonathan, she had thought of her emotions toward him as more spiritual and intellectual. But now she realized that in the months she had been under his spell, this physical closeness was part of what she had been longing for.

"My darling," he murmured, "I've wanted you for so long." Eagerly he lifted her onto his lap, balancing her across his body. Swiftly his hands went to the buttons of her blouse.

That woke Rachel up. No matter what she felt toward him, Jonathan belonged to somebody else. "No," she moaned in protest, trying to push his invading hands away from her body. Somehow he had undone the buttons of his own shirt so that she could feel the smooth flesh of his chest against her own naked skin. His insistent hand was now on the sensitive skin of her inner thigh, arousing in her a strong sensual response, but she couldn't allow this to go on. Yet, despite her attempts to push him away, he wouldn't stop. Lost in her own confusing swirl of sensations and emotions, she didn't hear the office door open. Desperately fighting her own weakness, she was about to beg Jonathan to stop when Dr. Mauberry, dean of the College of Arts and Sciences, cleared his throat.

"Well," he snapped. "I see I'm interrupting some rather important research. So if you'll just excuse me. . . ." As she looked around, her horrified glance caught the cold condemnation in the older man's eyes. She felt as though ice water had been dashed in her face. Without another word he withdrew from the room. And Jonathan, shaken and pale, scrambled to his feet and began to put himself back together as quickly as possible.

Thinking back on that moment now, Rachel's cheeks flamed with mortification. But if that few seconds of discovery had been horrible, her interview the next day with the dean had been far worse.

She was given to understand that only because the semester was so far advanced would she be allowed to finish the year and get her degree. And the decision to give up her research duties with Professor Convers was made for her.

Rachel had expected to be offered a position at the university the next year; she hadn't even applied to any other schools. Now she had to scurry to send out transcripts and applications. She knew the incident with Jonathan affected her letter of recommendation from the dean, who obviously regarded her as a tramp. Her only recourse had been to send Jonathan a brief note requesting his help. And he had responded with a glowing letter praising her academic work and research skills. It had been a major factor in securing the job at Quincy Adams at the last minute.

Yet, Jonathan avoided her during those last weeks before summer vacation. And she gave his office a wide berth too. Still in shock over what had happened, she was too embarrassed and confused to want to see him. And she thought she understood why he didn't seek her out. If the story had got around, it could have cost him tenure. But still, if he had cared anything for her, wouldn't he have called to apologize or explain?

Rachel had been unable to keep herself from brooding over the incident with Jonathan. Her mind ran it over and over like a caged squirrel racing futilely on an exercise wheel. And the more she thought about it, the more importance it assumed. She let her anguish, humiliation, and disillusionment burn her emotions raw. And finally she convinced herself that there was no way she could face the prospect of such pain again. Though she told herself she was no longer in love with Jonathan, she was still obsessed with her idealized memory of him. And so her instinct for self-preservation had made her discourage other relationships that seemed threatening to her. She rationalized to

35

herself that if by chance she ever sought out a man, she would look primarily for gentleness and companionship. The intense emotion she had felt for Jonathan was too dangerous to risk again.

Now she stared with horror at Jason Brand's ruined journal protruding from her garbage can. There was one thing she knew for sure: A man like him had no place in her life. She had been wary of him before. Now she would have to be on her guard every minute.

CHAPTER THREE

It was more than an hour before Rachel could calm down enough to think rationally after she had destroyed Jason Brand's journal.

She could just imagine what Charles Riddle would say if she went to him with a complaint about Brand. He would laugh at her; the whole English department would have a field day laughing at her. And that was probably what Jason Brand wanted. At first, she knew, he had simply been interested in her sexually. Rachel was no longer the naive little graduate student who had trembled in Jonathan Convers's arms. She was now quite capable of interpreting Jason Brand's caressing scrutiny. But his attitude had changed since her indiscretion in the cafeteria. She had stung his ego; now he wanted to get back at her. But she was not stupid enough to fall into his little trap. Her best course was to ignore him. Maybe, if he couldn't get a rise out of her, he would get bored, drop the class, and leave her in peace.

When the writer came sauntering up to her desk to collect his journal, she smiled sweetly at him.

"Oh, Mr. Brand," she purred, lowering her eyelashes to hide her expression. "I'm afraid I have a terrible confession to make."

A wary smile hovered around the corners of his mouth while he surveyed her downcast eyes with interest. "Yes?"

"I'm afraid I never read your journal. On my way home with it, I tripped and dropped it into a storm sewer. So clumsy of me. It was quite ruined by the muck." She opened her thick dark lashes wide and gave him a look of helpless appeal, her large eyes limpid, like pools of spring water. "I'm desolated not to have read what you wrote. I'm sure it was terribly clever and original. I beg your pardon, and I do hope you forgive me."

Hooking a hand over his hip pocket, Jason Brand cocked his head to one side, an arrested expression on his lean, aquiline face. His eyes gleamed like blue gunmetal, and a slow, fascinated smile began to form on his sensual mouth.

"Ms. Pritchard, there's very little I won't forgive you." He paused, then added in a low, teasing voice, "If you beg me." The smile became brilliant, flashing across his dark face like a searchlight. "I liked hearing you beg my forgiveness," he went on lightly, obviously enjoying himself. "It made my whole day."

Jason Brand might be able to treat the exchange as some sort of highly entertaining game, but Rachel couldn't. Her eyes turned flinty, and her jaws clamped together. But, still grinning broadly, Brand had turned and sauntered out the door.

After that, Rachel's awareness of him intensified. During class she was always conscious of his eyes on her. It was actually a physical sensation; her skin prickled with it. And now that she had an idea of what he was thinking, sometimes her legs would become so rubbery, she would have to steady herself against the blackboard.

As the days crawled by she found the situation more and more intolerable. In the beginning she had only to worry about encountering Jason Brand's speculative stare in class. But after the journal episode he was suddenly everywhere: She was constantly running into him hobnobbing with students in the halls; chatting with faculty members in their offices; and draped familiarly over the secretaries' desks, his smiles oozing charm and his dark blue eyes sparkling with mischief.

No one but Rachel objected to what she considered this relentless, calculating invasion. In fact, everyone appeared flattered. She was the only one in school who seemed to dislike him. People were constantly telling her how lucky she was to have him in her class. Even Marta was taken in.

"He's really charming," she had informed Rachel one afternoon. "You ought to have heard the discussion a group of students and I had with him about the New York literary scene. He had us all in stitches with his stories about Roosevelt Wolfhead and those other crazy writers you're always reading about. Would you believe Wolfhead actually rented ad space on the New York subway to lodge a complaint against his editor?"

"You're kidding," Rachel choked out between spurts of laughter. "If we tried that with Riddle, we'd probably all get fired."

Marta was eager to turn the subject back to Jason Brand. "You're the one who gets to spend the most time with our star pupil. How's it going?"

39

Rachel shrugged noncommittally and looked down at the polished tips of her black pumps. "Still down on him, I see," Marta observed. "I don't understand what you have against him. He's won over everyone else, especially the students. He spends a lot of time with them, you know, listening to their problems and offering suggestions."

Rachel stared at her friend. Were they talking about the same man? If Marta could only see the journal entry Jason Brand had written, she would change her tune. But that was impossible. Rachel had destroyed the evidence. And besides, her wariness of men was one of the few topics she had never felt comfortable discussing with Marta.

One day, as Rachel was retrieving the usual heap of mimeographed notices from her space in the nest of departmental mailboxes, a familiar deep male voice caught her attention. She swung her head abruptly and observed Jason Brand perched sideways on the English department secretary's desk. "Cathy, I like a girl with a rich fantasy life," he was saying with wry amusement, "but spelling *iridescent* three different ways on the same page is more creative than even I can approve of. Next time you do some typing for me, don't be afraid to use the dictionary when you're not sure," he said good-naturedly.

The girl reacted to his criticism as though to a compliment, returning his smile with a pleased flush. Just then Brand happened to glance up, catching Rachel's expression before she was able to swing away. His eyes brightened like reflective bits of glass, and his mouth curled while he winked at her in an intimate way that made her stiffen with annoyance.

Spinning on her heels, Rachel marched down the stairs toward her second-floor office. As she blindly turned the bend in the landing she ran headlong into Tom Metcalf, one of the new assistant professors.

Brought up short, the young man chuckled, his eyes admiring her flushed face as he seized her elbow to steady her. Tom was new this year. He had a ready, boyish smile, which he had used several times to strike up a conversation with Rachel.

"We have to stop meeting like this," he said, releasing her arm.

"What?" Rachel asked in confusion.

"Then you didn't bump into me on purpose?" Tom persisted, his eyes still warm as he regarded her quizzically, one pale brown eyebrow lifted.

"Oh, uh, no. . . . I'm sorry. I had my—my mind on something else," Rachel stammered.

"Were you thinking about the Kaufman lecture? That's what everybody seems to be talking about."

Rachel stared. It was a moment before she was able to take in his meaning. Then she remembered that tonight Dorothy Kaufman was giving a talk entitled "Women and the Cultural Ethos." Kaufman was a women's rights advocate with a national reputation as a writer and speaker. Her address was sponsored by the English department, and Professor Riddle had made it clear that the rank and file were expected to put in an appearance to swell the audience.

Rachel had planned to attend anyway. She had been an admirer of Dorothy Kaufman's for some time. But her mind hadn't been on the woman when she'd bumped into Tom.

Nevertheless, the lecture made a good excuse for her absentminded behavior.

"Actually I was wondering about what she was going to say," Rachel fibbed.

Metcalf's smile broadened. "I'm looking forward to it myself. Why don't we go together?"

Rachel opened her mouth to refuse. But then the young man's friendly expression made her reconsider. Why not, after all? she asked herself. He seemed like a harmless, pleasant sort. It was also time she came out of her cocoon. In fact, it was time she stopped feeling sorry for herself and started to have something like a normal social life. And Tom was just the safe sort of man it would be good to start with.

"I'd like that," she told him.

"Great!" he responded exuberantly. "I'll pick you up at seven thirty."

Rachel gave him directions to her apartment off MacArthur Boulevard and then continued to her office.

Before unlocking the door to her own cubicle, she glanced into Marta's. Her friend was bent over an untidy desk, scrawling comments in red ballpoint pen on a stack of papers. Her glasses had slipped halfway down her shiny nose, and her straight hair hung limply around her ears in dark points. Rachel suppressed a smile. Marta had a way of looking like she'd just been rescued from the *Titanic*.

Glancing up, the young woman interrupted Rachel's inadvertent appraisal and flung down her pen with uncharacteristic exasperation.

"These themes are impossible," she complained. "I don't know what I'm going to do. I can't give every kid in the class an F."

Rachel grinned sympathetically. "It must be taking a long time to make that decision. You don't usually start grading in the middle of the afternoon."

"No," Marta agreed wryly. "I usually put off starting on them until after dinner and half a pot of coffee. But I'm planning on going to the Kaufman lecture tonight, so I thought I'd try and get through them now. Want to go with me?"

Rachel made a disappointed face. "I wish you'd told me ten minutes ago. I just agreed to go with Tom Metcalf."

Marta's eyes sharpened oddly and then dropped back to her papers. "I thought you never dated faculty members," she mumbled. "But I can see why Tom might change your policy on that. He's very attractive."

Rachel stared at her friend in consternation. "I'd really rather go with you," she said earnestly. "But I am trying to make an effort this year to get out more, and Tom just came along at the right moment."

Marta nodded almost imperceptibly but didn't look up to meet her friend's eyes. Rachel stared at her bent head with concern. She sensed that she was causing Marta real distress, but she wasn't sure why. Could she really be that upset about having to go to the lecture alone?

"Listen," she suggested, trying to be helpful. "Why don't you ask Muffy? She might like to go."

Marta gave a snort of derisive laughter. "Somehow I don't think a militant feminist is Muffy's cup of tea. She's more interested in flirting with any attractive male she can find, attached or unattached. If she gets through this semester with her engagement ring still intact, I'll be surprised. Haven't you seen her floating around the department, perching on all their desks like a pet cockatoo?"

Rachel had to admit that what Marta said was true. The academic year was barely underway, but Muffy was already developing a reputation for availability.

"In one week that woman has gotten more male attention than I have all my life," Marta blurted with surprising bitterness. "And then there's you, Rachel," she added without looking up. "They notice you, and you don't even try. Why, I bet Tom Metcalf doesn't even know I exist. And he probably wouldn't ask me out unless I threatened him at gunpoint," she went on vehemently.

Rachel was startled. "Oh, Marta, I'm sure that isn't true," she protested. But the other woman only shot her a derisive look.

"You and I both know I'm destined to be the oldest living spinster freshman English instructor," she muttered fiercely, turning abruptly back to her papers.

Rachel hovered uneasily at the open door, her expression troubled. She wanted to say something consoling. But Marta's hunched shoulders and tight expression made that impossible. Finally she turned away and went back to her own office. She had planned to spend some time at her desk correcting themes, but now she scooped up the pile of compositions, shoved them into her briefcase, and headed out the door toward the parking lot.

The leaves were just beginning to turn. Glints of red and gold dappled the green masses, and even the late afternoon sun could not dispel the promise of autumn in the air. It was Rachel's favorite season, and usually she stared appreciatively at the trees as she walked. But now as she made her way to her car her mind was too distressed by Marta's outburst to dwell on the beauty of the campus.

The shortest route home was along Foxhall Road, a winding byway lined with huge old mansions interspersed with ultramodern dream houses—many visible only through a screen of evergreens. Often she amused herself by speculating about the monied Washington families who had built these palatial domiciles. But today the little scene with Marta was nagging at her mind. She hadn't realized her colleague was unhappy about her looks. What had triggered the uncharacteristic revelation?

"Why, I'll bet she likes Tom Metcalf," Rachel suddenly exclaimed aloud. That must be it. And Marta was right; he probably hadn't noticed her. With her dowdy appearance she just wasn't the kind of woman men noticed.

In her mind's eye Rachel conjured up an image of her friend. Actually, she thought, Marta could be pretty if she lost weight and dressed differently. She had lovely eyes; and with her hair cut properly to complement the bone structure of her face, she could look very good. Speculatively Rachel nibbled her bottom lip. She'd love to help with the makeover, if only Marta would let her.

She was still mulling over the problem that evening as she dressed for the Kaufman lecture. Thinking about Marta's appearance had made her think of her own. It had been months since she'd made any attempt to dress with flair. The decision to go out had given Rachel's spirits a surprising lift. She decided to forgo her usual teacher's uniform of tailored blouse and skirt in favor of rust-colored velvet designer jeans, a cream beige silk shirt, and a well cut tweed jacket.

Surveying herself in the mirror, she realized with pleasure that she felt young and carefree for the first time in ages. On an impulse she reached up and began to pull the confining pins from her hair. A few flicks of the brush and it was lying in loose waves around her slender shoulders.

Tom Metcalf's appreciative exclamation as he picked her up was her reward. "I'm going to have the best-looking lady in the lecture hall on my arm," he told her cheerfully. Rachel laughed, but she had to admit the compliment felt good.

45

When they entered the hall ten minutes before the program was to begin, the large room was only one-third full.

"This is a disgrace," Rachel muttered disgustedly into Tom's ear. "A woman this well-known and distinguished should be packing them in."

Tom shrugged. "I guess our students aren't sophisticated enough to appreciate Kaufman," he hedged, steering her toward an empty set of seats near the middle of the auditorium. "You have to admit, if you're not a feminist, she can be an acquired taste." Rachel shot him a half-amused glare.

In the next few minutes several dozen more students and English department members straggled in. But Marta was not among them. Apparently she had decided to forgo the lecture after all. Rachel felt a twinge of regret. Should she have asked Marta to come along with her and Tom? But no, she knew her friend would not have accepted the invitation.

Finally Charles Riddle and Dorothy Kaufman came out onto the stage. Just as the dapper, silver-haired chairman reached the lectern, two latecomers moved into the next row, blocking Rachel's view. Despite the fact that the whole row was empty, the couple picked the seats directly in front of Tom and Rachel.

She stared at them in astonishment. It was Jason Brand and Muffy Waddington. In a tawny gold corduroy jacket and tailored wool slacks, the writer looked lean, fit, and formidably attractive. Muffy, in an emerald silk shirtwaist, was the picture of feminine chic. Rachel's eyes shot to the woman's left hand. The ring was still there, winking like a searchlight. But apparently neither Muffy nor Jason Brand regarded it as a deterrent. As he pushed down his seat the writer slid Rachel an amused glance, his blue eyes

46

brightening as they lingered on her thick loosened hair. Suddenly she regretted having dressed so casually. Though it had not occurred to her that Jason Brand would attend the lecture, something in his expression suggested he believed she had worn her hair loose *solely* for his benefit. He smiled into her frosty eyes with maddening deliberation before turning to seat himself.

The writer had positioned himself so that she was going to be forced to stare at the back of his muscular neck for the entire lecture. Rachel looked around. But the seats on either side were taken. Even so, she would have suggested a shift to Tom, but it was too late. Dorothy Kaufman had already begun to speak.

Rachel did her best to concentrate on what the famous feminist was saying. But just as Kaufman began to outline her theory of culture, Muffy slid a silk-covered arm around her date's shoulder.

Rachel watched in fascination as Muffy's fingers crept toward Jason's strongly molded neck and began to play with the hair curling over the base of his collar. It was very obvious to Rachel that Muffy was more interested in Jason Brand than in Dorothy Kaufman. For his own part Brand showed no sign of reaction. But he also made no move to shake off the caressing fingers.

Tom leaned over to whisper in Rachel's ear. "This should be interesting. He's got a live one in Muffy!"

Rachel nodded grimly. There was no doubt about that.

The hand continued working over Jason Brand's nape in languorous stroking movements; finally the pale fingers with their polished nails slipped dexterously under the cuff of his white turtleneck. Was she planning to disrobe him in the lecture hall? Rachel wondered.

Involuntarily she shivered. She could almost imagine

what it would be like if her own fingers were touching that strong neck. She couldn't help herself. All the repressed sexual attraction she had felt toward Jason Brand day after day in class seemed to have been unleashed by this little scene with Muffy.

Dorothy Kaufman's words became just a background buzz. Despite herself, Rachel's attention remained riveted on the strong, brown column of Jason Brand's neck and the way his wide shoulders filled the back of the seat. For Rachel the rest of the lecture went by in a confused haze. She was hardly able to take in a word Dorothy Kaufman was saying.

When the ordeal was finally over, Rachel turned to Tom. "Do you mind if we go right to the reception?" she begged. "I don't want to mill around here." The truth was she didn't want to see the amusement deep in Jason Brand's cobalt-blue eyes. It may have been Muffy doing the caressing, but somehow she couldn't shake off the conviction that it had all been Jason Brand's fault.

Outside the cool evening air helped her regain some measure of calm. *What's the matter with me?* she asked herself in disgust. *I let Muffy and Jason Brand ruin a lecture I'd been looking forward to for a week.*

Tom pulled open the library door and ushered Rachel inside. A white table in the lobby was spread with an assortment of cheeses, crackers, and two-gallon jugs of wine flanked by plastic cups.

"The English department's usual splendid banquet," Tom remarked with good-humored irony.

Since they were among the first to arrive, they went directly to the table, where Tom poured her a glass of red wine and she selected a Wheat Thin to nibble on. While he chatted idly about the talk, the room began to fill with students and faculty. The buzz of conversation grew louder.

"They may not be great on culture, but they always show up for the refreshments," Tom commented wryly, looking at the students flocking around the cheese board.

Rachel nodded in agreement, but her mind was not on the students. She could hear a stir of excitement as the library doors opened and Charles Riddle ushered in the guest of honor. Dorothy Kaufman—a tall thin, distinguished-looking woman with shoulder-length salt and pepper hair—was deep in conversation with Jason Brand. Trailing the two writers was a disgruntled-looking Muffy. Clearly Dorothy Kaufman and Jason Brand were old friends. The well-known feminist was laughing up into Brand's blue eyes with a rapt expression.

The sight made Rachel turn away. Dorothy Kaufman was one of her heroines—with feet of clay, she could see now.

Hastily she bent to refill her glass. Before the lecture she had planned to try and approach Kaufman to tell her how much she admired her work. But now she discarded the idea.

Rachel spent the next ten minutes chatting idly with other faculty members. Finally beginning to feel claustrophobic from the press of bodies crowding around, she started looking for her escort. Would it be all right to ask Tom to take me home? she wondered. He was a nice guy, and she hated to spoil his evening, but she really didn't think she could stand much more of this. Her stomach was beginning to churn.

However, when she spotted Tom, she found, to her dismay, that he was talking to Jason Brand, looking up at the taller man with a mixture of self-conscious pleasure and awe. Her date's expression of boyish delight at being singled out by the campus celebrity was just too much to take. Threading her way through the milling crowd, she came up behind Tom and put her hand on his arm.

When he noticed her presence and turned to look down at her, she appealed, "I do have a lot of papers to grade, and I'm dead on my feet. Would you mind terribly if I asked you to take me home now?" As she spoke she was painfully conscious of Jason Brand's eyes on her, but she stubbornly refused to acknowledge his mocking glance.

Tom gave Rachel an imploring look. "I was just going to try and find you. Jason has invited us to stop off and have a drink at Strawberry Fields with him and Muffy." Rachel swallowed, feeling herself neatly trapped. It was obvious Tom definitely wanted to go. All her instincts urged her to insist he take her home first. Then she looked up and encountered the gleam in Brand's eyes. He was trying to make trouble, she guessed. But at the same time she felt it would be churlish of her to refuse.

"All right, but I really can't stay late," she added hesitantly.

Smiling with enthusiasm, Tom took her arm and began to lead her toward the exit. Rachel refused to look back to see whether Jason Brand and Muffy were following, and she let herself be led away.

But they were only a few steps behind. The two couples didn't part company until they arrived at the forsythia-lined parking lot, where Tom helped Rachel into his battered Honda. Jason Brand showed Muffy into his gleaming metallic-blue 280Z.

"See you at Strawberry Fields," Jason called smoothly before roaring off in his powerful sports car.

"You don't mind, do you?" Tom questioned half

apologetically as he headed out of the parking lot. "I read his book on the Special Forces. I was impressed, and I'd really like to hear more about his experiences."

Part of Rachel was tempted to come back with, "Well, I wouldn't." But she gave Tom a half-hearted smile and answered instead, "It's okay. Just so it's not too late an evening."

Tom smiled back in sympathy. "Yes, I know. Freshman English teachers always have papers to grade, even on the weekend. I don't know how you keep it up." Rachel made a face into the darkness. Sometimes she didn't know herself.

Strawberry Fields was in Georgetown. The route led along the C&O Canal, where mule-driven barges once brought goods from the Port of Georgetown to the midwest. Now the towpath was used by hikers and bicyclists, and the canal was a paradise for skaters in the winter.

They were soon in the heart of historic Georgetown with its Federal townhouses, brick-paved walkways, and shopping district filled with boutiques and interesting restaurants. Strawberry Fields was one of these. Jason Brand's sleek car was already parked in front of the red-brick building, but it took Tom several minutes to find a space on a nearby street. The entrance to the restaurant lounge was down a narrow cobblestone passageway flanked at either end by wrought-iron gates. When Tom had shepherded Rachel through the front door, they immediately spotted Jason Brand and his companion in a corner booth. The writer stood up when they entered; and after ushering Rachel onto the bench across from Muffy, he astonished Rachel by nonchalantly sliding in next to her instead of his own date.

As his hard thigh brushed hers Rachel felt sensual

51

awareness flicker through her body at the contact. Nervously she slid several inches away. Jason Brand shot her a knowing grin, and she blushed before looking quickly away, only to find herself confronting a furious Muffy. The blonde was shooting Rachel critical looks, as though she and not Jason Brand were somehow responsible for the awkward seating arrangement. On the other hand Tom did not seem particularly displeased. He slid in next to Muffy with a wide smile.

"Well, what shall we all have?" Brand drawled, ignoring the tension between the two women. "You ladies might like strawberry daiquiris. It's the specialty of the house."

"I'll have white wine," Rachel countered, moving to the far end of the bench. Muffy agreed to the daiquiri, and the two men ordered Scotch on the rocks.

Muffy looked coyly across at her date. "I didn't realize you were a friend of Dorothy Kaufman's. Somehow I wouldn't have thought she was your type," the blonde teased, wafting him a seductive look through her darkened lashes.

Jason leaned back, smiling dryly as he gave Muffy a comprehensive glance. "Who do you think is my type?"

How would Muffy know anything about Dorothy Kaufman? Rachel asked herself cynically. She certainly hadn't paid much attention to her this evening. And then, realizing that the same thing could be said of herself, Rachel felt color creep up her neck.

The corners of the blonde's full mouth curved up invitingly as she began to answer Jason Brand's question. "Oh, I picture you with someone less strident, a little softer, and more feminine."

The writer's grin widened, and then he surprised Rachel

by turning toward her and demanding, "And who do you think my type is?"

"Anything in skirts," Rachel found herself blurting before she'd had an opportunity to consider.

Jason barked a laugh while his blue eyes glinted down into hers. "Not far off," he admitted. "Though I often like them in pants even better." His eyes drifted down to Rachel's trouser-clad legs, and he slid an inch or two closer on the bench. To her horror she felt another stab of sensual excitement and pressed even closer to the wall. *This is ridiculous,* she thought, scolding herself; *I can't cower here like a trapped rabbit.* Quickly she adjusted her position slightly, although she was still careful to keep a distance between her own leg and Jason Brand's thigh.

"I like most women," the writer was saying. "But I particularly appreciate intelligent, independent women. So you see," he turned back toward Muffy, who was now visibly pouting, "Dorothy *is* my type. We're old friends, and I've been an admirer of hers for years."

Muffy's retort was interrupted by the waitress's serving the drinks. When she had bustled off, Tom leaned forward, obviously eager to resume the conversation the two men had begun at the reception.

"There's one thing you don't explain in your book on the Special Forces, and it's been bothering me," the young academic plunged in while Jason waited expectantly. "Why did you join up in the first place? It seems like such an unusual thing for a young man with your background to do, particularly growing up in the Sixties."

Brand's mouth twisted with grim amusement. "I think it was my background that did it," he admitted dryly. "My college professor father was the prototypical aging hippie—complete with long hair and love beads. He surrounded himself with flower children and whiled away the weekends going to peace demonstrations and volunteering for antidraft counseling." Jason Brand laughed humorlessly. "It gave the old man a real jolt when his son joined the Army and volunteered for special duty in Nam."

"What was your specialty?" Tom asked.

"Demolitions," Jason Brand replied crisply. "I always did like to see things go bang."

Rachel studied the salt shaker on the table in front of her. But in her mind's eye she was seeing Jason Brand's rigid profile in a new light. She had been picturing his father as a traditional straitlaced academic bedeviled by a wayward son. But Brand's startling revelation was forcing her to reinterpret the father-son relationship. How typical it was of the man, she thought, to pick a life-style so contrary to his father's.

But contrary or not, the whole idea of the Special Forces and the violence of the Vietnam War repelled her.

"The war was just a game for you," Rachel accused, projecting the full force of her disapproval into her voice.

Jason turned and met her gray stare head-on. "Most things in life are a game. But I didn't like the pointless violence, if that's what you mean."

"What was it that you liked?" Rachel persisted, unable to keep a belligerent edge out of her voice.

A faint smile twisted his mouth, and his blue eyes locked meaningfully with hers. "I didn't say I liked it. But there's merit in every experience. War sharpens your appreciation for life. Some people are content to be half dead. I like to be fully alive—in every possible way."

Rachel flushed, sensing the implicit accusation: the remark was too close to her own self-assessment for com-

54

fort. Hadn't she really been hiding from one very important part of life for the past year?

The man beside her pressed on relentlessly.

"War is inevitably an intense experience. You can't be so close to death and destruction without discovering how good it is to be alive. I didn't approve of the war, and I hope I'm never involved in another. Surely what I said about it in my book makes that clear. But I have to admit, I don't regret the experience. It forced me to appreciate the privilege of being able to see, hear, and touch the world as few other things could."

"You make yourself sound so hard-boiled," Tom interjected, "but you certainly haven't come across that way for the last few weeks on campus; and I've read you sponsor a fund for Vietnamese orphans. How does that fit into the hard-as-nails image?"

Rachel stared at Brand's profile, taking in the straight nose and the lean flat planes of his high cheekbones. Who was this man? He seemed like a puzzle. And none of the pieces she had picked up so far seemed to fit.

"It's something I prefer not to discuss," he was saying. "I'd like to strangle the reporter who got hold of that information." It was clear the topic was off limits.

A few moments later Jason looked at his watch and nodded to his date. "I think I'd better take you home. I know you need your beauty sleep," he told the blonde.

Muffy agreed with alacrity, obviously eager to be alone with him. Certainly the smile on her face suggested that she didn't expect to make an early night of it.

Rachel watched the couple leave the restaurant with barely concealed relief.

Turning back, she found Tom gazing at her wryly. "He's quite something," the young man ventured.

"Yes," Rachel agreed noncommitally. And then hastily she changed the subject.

They took the next twenty minutes to finish their drinks, chatting about Dorothy Kaufman and some of the faculty in the English department. Rachel was able to give Tom some tips on how to steer a safe course through the minefield of departmental politics.

Tom smiled gratefully at her as he paid the bill and escorted her back to his tiny car.

Should I say something about Marta? Rachel wondered, but decided against it.

As they neared her apartment Rachel began to wonder how she would handle the end of the evening. Tom probably expected a good-night kiss. But that was the last thing Rachel felt in the mood for. She was so preoccupied that she only half noticed the sleek sports car parked a few yards away from her modest building.

Tom's Honda had barely ground to a halt before Rachel had turned to unlock her door.

"Thank you for suggesting the lecture," she told her escort as she fumbled with the handle.

Tom grinned. "I was planning to walk you to the front door, you know. But I take it you'd prefer to find your own way."

Rachel flushed, realizing that Tom was receiving the brunt of her irritation with Jason Brand and that she wasn't being fair to him.

"Tom," she began hesitantly, "I do like you, and I'd like to be your friend. But right now I can't go beyond that with anybody."

Tom made a face. "All right. I get the message, and I won't pry. But I'll stay here until you're safely inside your apartment door."

"Thanks for understanding." Rachel gave his extended hand a quick squeeze and turned to go. In a moment she had gained the entrance to the building, where she waved to the young man in the car. As he pulled away she turned and headed up the metal and cement stairway that led to her second-floor apartment.

After slipping her key into the lock and letting herself in, she sighed with relief. Well, that was over. She took off her jacket and sat down in the overstuffed chair in the corner near the window. The evening had been much more of a strain than she had anticipated, and she was tired.

Pulling off her boots, she padded into the bedroom, where she doffed her slacks and shirt. Too tired to put on a nightgown, she stretched out on the bed in her lacy beige panties and wisp of a bra. Closing her eyes for a moment, she let her thoughts drift aimlessly. But she was startled out of her reverie by a sharp knock at the door.

Rachel's eyes snapped open. Could that be Tom? Had she left something in the car he wanted to return?

Sighing, she got up, snatched the Chinese silk robe from the back of her chair, and went to the door.

"Who is it?" she called out cautiously, belting the red silk tightly around her narrow waist.

There was a short pause. And then a low-pitched voice said, "It's Jason. Can I come in? I want to talk to you."

Rachel drew back, shocked. Jason Brand was the last person she expected at this hour. "No," she whispered hoarsely. "Go away."

"Let me in," the voice persisted in forcefully persuasive tones. "I think it's time we talked."

As he spoke Jason Brand twisted the doorknob, and Rachel stared at it in horror, wondering if the elderly gossip next door could hear him. *"Talked?"* she blurted out with considerable disbelief in her voice.

There was a pause and then a chuckle. "All right, you guessed it. I'd like to do more than talk. But if you'll let me in, I think we can manage to have a civilized conversation."

Rachel's eyebrows drew together. How were her neighbors reacting to this conversation? Tentatively she touched the doorknob. Should she let him in?

And then pride stiffened her shoulders. She was acting like a frightened little girl. But she was a grown woman, and she was not going to let this man think that she was afraid to be alone with him. She could handle Jason Brand.

Decisively Rachel clicked the lock and swung the door open. Staring up at him with an unconsciously defiant expression on her face, she stood aside, and the writer strolled into her tiny living room. It was odd how, now that she was alone with him, he suddenly seemed even larger than she remembered. His tall, muscular frame made the walls and ceiling constrict; and as he loomed over her Rachel felt a tightness in her throat as well.

He stood for a moment, lazily surveying the apartment, his hands jammed casually into his pants pockets. And she couldn't pull her eyes away from the wide shoulders and broad expanse of muscle under the finely tailored corduroy material of his jacket.

Then he half turned and smiled. His eyes glinted appreciatively at Rachel's flushed face and then began to gleam as they drifted down to caress the cleft of her breasts just visible at the closure of the red silk robe.

"Very nice," he drawled. "Your decor, I mean."

Rachel turned scarlet and clutched at the borders of her

silky dressing gown. All at once she wondered if she could really handle this situation and began to regret having let him in. But it was too late to order him out the door now. Jason Brand had the proprietary look of a man who had every intention of staying.

Something of her feelings must have shown in her face.

"What are you afraid of, Rachel?" he asked almost gently. "Is it what I wrote in the journal? I was angry then. And I apologize. But I'm feeling something quite different now. I want to get to know you."

Rachel reacted defensively. "I'm not afraid of anything," she began to deny. "It's late. I'm tired and I want to go to bed." But as she said the last words she felt her skin heat again, realizing how he would certainly take them.

"I—I mean," she hurried on, ignoring the slow grin spreading across his aquiline features, "I'm not accustomed to entertaining students in my apartment at this hour."

"When do you entertain your students, Ms. Pritchard?" he questioned, a laugh just at the edge of his voice. "I might as well tell you now that I'm not going to wait till the end of the semester to find out."

Rachel took a step backward. "I told you my rules about that."

Jason Brand shook his head slowly and moved toward her with calm deliberation. "But rules are made to be broken, Rachel. Besides, you told me you weren't afraid of anything." The blue eyes looked squarely into hers. "Did you mean that?"

Rachel opened her mouth, but no words came. She was too busy taking in the purposeful expression on Jason

Brand's face. A half smile quirked his well-shaped mouth as he slowly closed the remaining distance between them.

"Rachel," he murmured huskily, "when I came in here, I really did mean to have a conversation. But seeing you the way you are in that robe, with your hair around your shoulders—" He shook his head. "I can no more just stand around here talking to you than I could fly."

As if in slow motion, she watched his arms reach out. And then they were around her body, pressing her slender frame to the long hard expanse of his own.

One sun-browned hand began to stroke the sensitive skin at the back of her neck while the other pressed against her spine, burning through the thin material of her robe.

"Please, Jason," she tried weakly to protest. But the warmth of his insistent lips on hers stopped the words. Had it been a violent kiss, Rachel would have struggled to break free. But the tender exploration of his mouth on hers made her melt into his arms. Her body was suddenly alive with sensations. She could feel the rough material of his wool slacks prickling through the slick vulnerability of her robe, the buttons of his jacket pressing against her breasts, and most of all the exquisite delight of his warm lips taking possession of hers as he deepened the kiss.

It was such a skillful attack on her senses that for a moment she was completely unable to think. Her lips parted helplessly as she returned the kiss. And her body seemed to liquefy in his arms, molding itself to his narrow hips and the unyielding wall of his chest. Her own arms had slipped around his broad shoulders to pull him even more tightly against her.

She felt the fingers of his hand twine themselves possessively in her hair. And then his lips moved to her cheek, her closed eyelids, her forehead, and finally her ear where his tongue traced a delicate path around the outer shell. The delicious sensation made her shiver slightly.

"I've been wanting to do that ever since I first saw you," he muttered thickly. "That, and a lot more."

Rachel did not respond. It was as though she were in a sensual trance, unable to think or speak. The truth was she'd been wanting him to do this too. Secretly, she had imagined what the intimate touch of his hands and lips would be like. And now she knew. It was devastating!

Jason had tilted her head back and his warm lips were on her throat, exploring the hollow where her pulse throbbed wildly. Involuntarily, she groaned and Jason made an answering noise of satisfaction deep in his throat.

"Do you have any idea what you do to me?" he whispered.

While her dazed brain tried to make sense of what was happening, he arched her back and she felt his mouth travel a slow, tantalizing path down her quivering flesh to the cleft where the edges of her silk robe met. His free hand stroked softly down the side of her body, lightly grazing the fullness of her breasts and then moving to take possession of the soft mounds that now strained against the red silk. Jason's thumb toyed lightly with a firm nipple, and for a moment Rachel succumbed to the exquisite pleasure of the caress. But her own response was as much a warning to caution as an invitation to let herself be swept away on a tide of feeling. Opening passion-darkened eyes, Rachel tried to drag herself back to some semblance of sanity. But not until his hand began to slip the red silk garment off her shoulder did the cool air feathering her fevered skin finally wake her up, and all the heated passion Jason Brand had just aroused in her drained away in a reaction of fear.

"No," she gasped, bringing up her hands and pushing them against his chest with an emotion close to hysteria.

The protest made his body stiffen, and then he released her. Taking a step away, he stood looking down at her inquiringly. "What's wrong, Rachel?" he demanded. "A moment ago you wanted the same thing I did."

"That's not true," she denied furiously, pulling her robe securely about her shoulders. "You said we were going to have a civilized conversation. And I took you at your word. Now get out of here."

"I think we both know that what's between us demands more than a conversation."

"There's nothing between us," she sputtered, almost incoherent in her anger and nervous reaction. Did this man have the gall to think that he need only grab her, and she would fall into bed with him as easily as a ripe peach falls from a tree?

She glared up at him: all her outrage was written across her face, plain for him to see.

Jason surveyed her expression ruefully. "You're too upset for me to stay; I can see that. But whatever you're telling yourself now, you wanted me a moment ago as much as I wanted you. Don't kid yourself that you can build a wall by putting on this kind of an act, Rachel. What's been between us from the start is too real for that. And I've always been very good at knocking down walls." And without another word, he turned and strode out of the room, shutting the door with a firm but muffled click behind him.

Rachel sagged into a chair. She was shaking uncontrollably. She had escaped from Jason Brand tonight. But how was she going to face him on Monday in class?

CHAPTER FOUR

The next morning Rachel stared morosely into the black depths of her morning coffee cup: she wasn't in the mood for cream and sugar. The night before had been a restless one, and she needed to banish its effects.

"Get a grip on yourself, Rachel Pritchard," she muttered, and then took a strengthening sip of the hot black liquid. She'd been so upset after Jason Brand had finally left, that she'd paced the floor for more than an hour. And then, when she'd got into bed, she'd tossed and turned for hours.

Last night she'd assured herself that she could handle the man. And she'd brushed aside her fears and insecurities long enough to open the door. But, once they were alone, the undeniable magnetism of Jason Brand had made her body turn traitor.

Thank goodness she'd come to her senses before allowing him to maneuver her into bed. *He's probably only chasing me because I've given him the cold shoulder,* she

63

reasoned. *He must see me as some sort of challenge. And if I start believing him now, I'll only leave myself open for trouble, the way I did with Jonathan.*

Rachel shivered and pulled the Chinese robe closer around her shoulders. She couldn't help remembering the sensations Jason Brand had aroused when his potent hands had caressed her fevered skin. It was undeniable that, having caught her alone and off guard, the man had kindled a powerful response in her. But he wasn't going to get a chance to do it again. *That's the last time I let Jason Brand talk me into being alone with him,* she vowed, crossing her arms in front of her chest and setting her jaw. From now on it's strictly a classroom relationship.

It was just then that she became aware of a shaft of bright morning sunlight spilling in a pool around her coffee cup. Glancing up, she looked out the small window over her sink and saw that the sky was an invitingly brilliant blue against the gold-and-red tips of trees just visible from her chair. It was going to be a perfect autumn day. And it would be a crime to let thoughts of Jason Brand spoil it. Why not see if Marta wanted to go out somewhere?

But as Rachel's hand reached for the telephone receiver she suddenly remembered yesterday's scene in her friend's office. Maybe Marta was still upset. After all, she hadn't come to the lecture. And perhaps she would still want to keep her distance from Rachel today.

Well, the only way you're going to find out is to call, Rachel told herself, beginning to dial the familiar number. The other young woman answered after only the second ring; and a few moments into the conversation, Rachel's fears evaporated.

"I was just going to call you and suggest that we go out

somewhere," her friend exclaimed in her usual bubbly tones. "It's such a gorgeous day." She hesitated for a moment and then added, "That is, unless you have other plans."

"I have no plans at all," Rachel assured her, wondering if by *other plans* Marta was thinking about Tom. Maybe today she could make some subtle suggestions about how Marta could improve her appearance.

As it turned out, Marta seemed to be more than open to Rachel's hesitantly broached opinions. In fact, she even brought the subject up herself while they strolled along the boxwood-flanked brick paths of Georgetown's famous Dumbarton Oaks gardens.

"Rachel, you always look so terrific," she plunged in. "I know a lot of it is natural beauty. But are there any secrets you'd be willing to pass along to a less fortunate friend?"

Rachel turned around to stare at her companion. "Marta," she began, "Mother Nature didn't do so badly by you either. You've just been ignoring your gifts."

Her friend gave a self-derisive snort. "Like what, for instance?" she challenged.

"Like your beautiful eyes and your sparkling personality," Rachel countered. "Marta, you've got more wit and charm than any other woman I know."

"But no one gets to the personality because they're so put off by the rest of me," Marta pointed out, gesturing ruefully at her overgenerous proportions, which were disguised once again in a shapeless tent-dress.

This, Rachel knew, was the opening she had been looking for. And she plunged in with enthusiasm. "You've got a perfect hourglass figure, Marta," she pointed out. "There's just a little too much of it. If you just cut out that morning box of glazed doughnuts you always have around your office—"

"But I need energy to face the freshman horde," Marta objected.

"Believe me, you'll get more energy from cottage cheese and fresh fruit than from refined sugar," Rachel insisted. "And how about letting me show you around the university gym? I've been using the weight room for months now, and it's made a whole dress size difference for me."

"It has?" Marta exclaimed, her eyebrows shooting up to her hairline. "I always thought weightlifting gave you bulging muscles."

Rachel shook her head. "No, a few sessions every week in the circuit weight room just firm you up and make you feel good."

Marta was staring at her openmouthed. "And here I always figured a size nine was your birthright, while I was stuck with a sixteen for life."

Rachel grinned and shook her head. "You don't know how many doughnuts I've turned down in the name of prudence," she laughed. "I feel so much better at this weight that it's worth sacrificing the goodies."

Marta gazed at her friend with new respect. "I didn't realize you had so much willpower, Rachel," she admitted. "I don't know if I could match you on that. I've always eaten what I wanted because men never paid attention to me anyway, and I figured it was hopeless. But maybe I've got a good enough reason now to give it a real try."

Rachel eyed Marta speculatively. Was that "good enough reason" Tom? But she had too much tact to come out and ask. Instead, she looked at her friend with understanding and squeezed her hand. "Let's go have a light lunch," she said, underlining the *light* with a mischievous smile. "And talk this whole thing over seriously."

They had lunch at a little restaurant on Wisconsin Avenue that featured elaborate salads and health-food sandwiches. While the two women munched on alfalfa sprouts, tomatoes, and crisp raw vegetables, they worked out a diet and exercise strategy for Marta.

"You don't want to lose too fast," Rachel cautioned after they had paid the check, "but it's nice to get off to a good start." Then the slender redhead snapped her fingers. "I know. Let's stop by one of those boutiques at Georgetown Mall and get you a gorgeous dress two sizes too small. At the prices they charge there, that should be real incentive to stick to your diet."

Marta chuckled appreciatively. "Rachel, you're always full of tricks."

And with that the twosome set off for the posh shopping mall bordering the canal.

"I've always felt intimidated by this place," Marta confessed as she pulled open one of the polished wood and frosted glass doors. Like the rest of Georgetown Mall, it positively radiated Victorian elegance.

"Just pretend you're a character out of Oscar Wilde," Rachel suggested, "and sweep grandly down the promenades as if you had all the money in the world."

Marta giggled doubtfully. "It may take all the money in the world to buy a dress here. Maybe we should have gone to a discount department store instead."

"Absolutely not," Rachel chided. "A bargain-basement dress won't be any incentive to stick with your diet. Besides, think of all the free atmosphere you get here." She gestured expansively at the tiers of wrought-iron balconies, massive chandeliers, and banks of potted palms.

The mall housed a wide selection of tempting boutiques designed for browsing and window-shopping. But Marta was right. The prices were unbelievable. Though the two women strolled through several shops looking at tweedy sports togs, sophisticated daytime dresses, and stunning evening wear, all items of clothing boasted astronomical price tags.

As they rounded a corner, however, they came upon a little salon selling stylishly appealing lingerie. Recently opened for business, it was in the midst of an introductory sale. Featured in the window were several delicately feminine teddies. And Rachel, who had a weakness for lacy lingerie, was struck by their romantic charm.

"You'd have to feel sexy in one of these," she whispered to Marta. "And they're on sale too."

"I'd look like a sausage that was much too big for its casing," her friend countered. "So price isn't even a factor."

"Not after your diet and exercise program you won't, so let's get you one instead of a dress," Rachel suggested. "A mental picture of the new Marta lounging around in one of those will keep you on the right track for sure."

As she spoke she stepped into the shop. And Marta followed.

An assortment of whisper-sheer teddies in soft lavenders, grays, pinks, yellows, whites, and even daring black took up one wall of the small boutique. They looked a bit like camisoles with panties.

Rachel pulled out a silken gray one edged with lace and held it out to Marta. "Imagine wearing this under a strait-laced teaching outfit," she suggested wickedly.

Marta blushed. But she reached out to caress the soft material between her thumb and fingers.

68

"Maybe I will get one," she said, and then broke into a broad grin. "But only if you do too, Rachel."

It was something that neither woman would have done on her own. But with each egging the other on, they spent almost half an hour picking among the wispy garments. Marta finally settled on a shell-pink model two sizes too small. And Rachel selected one in a subtle shade of peach with bands of beige lace edging the bodice and legs and a row of tiny buttons down the front.

"I don't know when I'm going to wear this," she confided to Marta as she waited for the sales clerk to return her credit card.

"Oh, I'm sure the opportunity will come up," her friend assured.

A frown creased Rachel's forehead. The comment might have been an opening to talk about her evening with Jason Brand. After all, hadn't she and her friend spent the morning sorting out Marta's life? But somehow Rachel wasn't in the mood to focus on herself. As close as she felt to Marta, her own tangled emotions were just too painful to confide. And she had to admit that what she'd been doing all day was concentrating on Marta's welfare in order to hold her own problems at bay.

But when Rachel said good-bye to her friend later that day and found herself alone again in her apartment, all of her worries came out of their hiding places in a rush. Just how was she going to face Jason Brand? Could she pretend that nothing had happened between the two of them? Would his presence make it impossible for her to teach effectively?

She was still nervously turning these questions over in her mind when she pulled open the door of her classroom Monday morning. Her eyes shot involuntarily to the corner of the room where the writer always sat. His chair was empty. To her chagrin, she felt a little stab of disappointment. Why hadn't he come today? Was he avoiding her too?

It was something she was forced to ask herself over and over in the days that followed, for Jason Brand did not put in an appearance in her class all week. As the days passed, Rachel found that part of her mind couldn't help worrying about him. Running away just wasn't his style. At odd moments frightening scenes would leap into her mind: Jason's car smashed against a tree or toppling over the railing of a bridge; Jason trapped in the car wreck or unconscious and pale in a hospital bed.

Stop being ridiculous, she told herself firmly. There's nothing wrong with the man. A rejection from you hasn't driven him over the edge. But where was he, then? Finally she was able to convince herself that he had simply dropped Freshman Comp. However, no form arrived in her departmental mailbox; and she was reluctant to ask the department secretary about the matter. Despite all her firm admonitions, she found herself scanning the faces in the Faculty Club and peering anxiously at the groups of students hurrying across campus to get out of the late October wind. But Jason Brand's tall muscular body and leonine head seemed to have disappeared. And Rachel felt a curious emptiness as she acknowledged that perhaps she wouldn't be seeing him again.

The next week private student-conferences were scheduled in place of regular classes, and Rachel busied herself going through student folders and making notes on what she wanted to discuss with each member of her class. When she walked into the anteroom of her office on the second day of conferences, she was astonished to see Jason

70

Brand lounging against the wall, exchanging good-humored banter with several Freshman Comp students. Though he had signed up for the two P.M. slot weeks before, she had not expected him to appear.

Looking up just in time to catch her incredulous expression, he grinned. "Well, hello, Ms. Pritchard. Did you miss me?" he queried impudently.

All of the worry she had felt in his absence suddenly transformed itself into anger. But it was an anger that Rachel's pride would not allow her to show.

"Oh, we managed to get along without you," she tossed breezily over her shoulder as she turned to unlock her office. Shutting the door behind her, she set her briefcase carefully on the floor and hung her coat up on the rack in the corner. But as she went through the automatic movements she was fuming. The nerve of the man! He'd made her imagination run wild. And now here he was back, as if he'd never been away. Sitting down and putting her fingertips on the desk top, she took several deep breaths. Calm down, she told herself. Don't let him do this to you. But it was only by sheer force of will that she was able to put Jason Brand out of her mind for the moment and concentrate on the task at hand.

Her first interview of the afternoon was with Phil Dugan—a boy who seemed to understand the basics of grammar, spelling, and punctuation, but whose writing unfortunately showed no real spark of creativity. Rachel ruffled through the rack of student folders at the back of her desk until she found Phil's. She had already marked a number of passages where more effective phrasing could be used. And she wanted to go over them with him during the half-hour session.

At precisely one thirty the young man tapped hesitantly

71

on the heavy wooden door separating her private cubicle from the anteroom.

"Come in," she called out. "And shut the door behind you."

It was obvious from the way the boy fidgeted in his folding chair and looked at a spot on the wall near her left shoulder that Phil was nervous about the conference. Rachel did her best to put him at ease by starting with the strong points of his performance. And as she gradually began to bring in some of her criticisms, she let him come up with his own ideas for improvements. It was often an effective teaching tool, she had learned, because the student could see himself making headway.

"Look at this passage," she suggested, pointing to the second page of an essay. "You call the soldier's uniform 'tight.' Could you think of an image that would help the reader see the picture?"

"An image?" Phil replied.

"Yes. Maybe his uniform was as tight as, say, a second skin. Or tight as a diver's wet suit," Rachel improvised.

The boy thought for a minute. "Or maybe tight as a pair of wet blue jeans?"

Rachel smiled encouragingly. "Yes, that's the idea." They went on to several more passages, and Rachel was pleased with how well Phil picked up the idea.

"I never thought of using stuff like that in an essay, Ms. Pritchard," he admitted as the half-hour session drew to a close. "But I will from now on." Pushing back his chair, he stood up. "Shall I ask the next student to come in?" he questioned politely.

Rachel nodded, feeling her body tense. The next student, she knew, was Jason Brand. With hands that suddenly felt enclosed in thick leather gloves, she turned and began to fumble for his folder. Her back was still to the entrance when she heard Philip leave. And she hadn't yet turned back to face the room when she heard the heavy door being shut firmly.

Whirling around, she came face to face with the writer. He leaned casually against the jamb, one hand thrust into the pocket of his brown cords and the other holding a notebook identical to the one she had burned three weeks ago. As he took in her startled expression a lazy smile spread across his handsome features.

"Surely you were expecting me, Ms. Pritchard," he chided gently, crossing the small room and laying the journal on her desk. He smiled wickedly into her eyes. "And I know you wouldn't want to miss another fascinating installment in my journal, assuming that you really did read the first one, that is."

Rachel pointedly ignored the remark and the notebook. "But you were away all week. I didn't really think you'd be back," she blurted, more for her own benefit than his.

"You've hurt my feelings. I thought you knew I'd travel through fire and floods to keep an appointment with you."

Though his words made her ears burn, Rachel forced a sardonic laugh. "Now, really, that's preposterous." She wasn't going to let Jason Brand get the better of her—not this time, not in her office. If he wanted to discuss his classwork, that was fine. But she wasn't going to be trapped into a half hour of inane banter. And she wasn't going to let him make her angry either. She was absolutely determined that this was going to be a businesslike encounter between teacher and student.

Now that they were alone together, however, she couldn't help feeling an intense awareness of his physical presence. But this time, she told herself, she wasn't going

73

to be intimidated by his sexual magnetism. She was going to ignore the challenging glint in his blue eyes; the ripple of muscle under his tan turtleneck as he turned a metal chair to face hers; and the faint, oddly seductive tang of his after-shave wafting toward her across the three feet that now separated them.

Opening his folder, she began to flip through the pages in what she hoped was a professional-looking way. But there was a problem with her plan. Since she hadn't been expecting the writer, she wasn't really prepared to discuss his work.

"Uh, did you want my comments on any particular essays?" she began, not daring to lift her gray eyes to Jason Brand's hard-chiseled features. The touch of his gaze as it drifted over her face made her nerves jump.

"I think your comments were quite adequate," he countered, an undercurrent of amusement in his deep voice.

But Rachel wasn't willing to let him control the situation. "Well, if you like, we could discuss some of your other works—your books, for example."

"Oh? I hadn't imagined that you'd made a study of my writing," he confessed. "Were you trying to 'know thy enemy'?"

He wants to goad me, Rachel thought, struggling to hang on to her polite professorial demeanor. *But I'm not going to let him.* "Why, Mr. Brand," she countered sweetly, looking up now to meet the blue probe of his eyes, "you don't mean to imply that the two of us are enemies, do you?"

He turned his dark head, and sunlight from her office window played over the strong line of his cheeks and jaw, sharpening the impact of his male good looks. "Certainly

74

not," he denied. "What facets of my work did you want to discuss?"

If I can just keep this literary conversation going, he'll be out of here in another twenty minutes, Rachel thought desperately. "Uh, well, I had noticed that your books skimp a bit on background," she asserted.

"Go on," he invited, arching a dark eyebrow and leaning back in his chair. Stretching out his long legs with loose-limbed grace, he crossed them comfortably at the ankles, making Rachel devastatingly aware of the leanness of his hips and the broadness of his shoulders under the turtleneck pullover he wore.

"Well, take your book on Vietnam, for example. You tell us a lot about attitudes toward that war. But the reader has to make his own comparisons. If he doesn't know about the extreme patriotism generated by World Wars One and Two, he misses a lot."

Jason Brand's blue eyes were fixed on her face, and for a moment Rachel felt as if two laser beams were boring into her head. Suddenly she regretted the criticism. What did she know really? The man's books were published, and hers were still sitting in a desk drawer.

"I didn't mean—" She tried to back off.

But he shook his head. "No, you're right. I've noticed myself that I tend to focus so tightly on my subject that I slight the background. Angelique and I have talked about it."

"Angelique?"

"My editor at Fanfare Books. She's quite a woman. We spent the week at her place in Connecticut, talking about the concept for this book on Quincy Adams—and plans for the future."

"Her place?" Rachel asked stupidly. Nothing about this conference was going the way she had expected.

Jason Brand nodded, warming to his subject. "Yes. We covered a tremendous amount. She had some marvelous ideas about some of the later chapters, and even suggested that I flesh them out—add more background, as you put it—by making some research trips to other colleges. It will make the Quincy Adams experience less isolated." But Rachel hardly heard his words. All week she had wondered where he was. And now she knew—with another woman. What a stupid fool she'd been to actually worry about the man when he was obviously so well taken care of. Devastating images of the unknown Angelique began to flash through her imagination.

"I'll just bet you covered a tremendous amount," she bit out, jumping to her feet and glaring down at him in a way that made a mockery of the cool, professional manner she had just schooled herself to assume. "Do you expect me to believe that you spent the weekend working?"

As he took in her agitation, the blue of his eyes changed to the deep indigo of a storm-tossed ocean. In one fluid motion he was out of his own chair and reaching for her. As she stood rooted to the spot, horrified by the words that had just tumbled out of her mouth, he took her roughly by the shoulders, his fingers pressing through the thin material of her blouse with bruising intensity.

"Ms. Pritchard," he ground out, "I believe I am not required to justify my every move to my Freshman Composition teacher. And as for what you think, I believe you have a very limited perspective from which to judge what goes on between a man and a woman—no matter how perceptive your judgments in literary matters."

While he spoke Rachel tried to twist away from his

grasp. But his hands on her shoulders held her firmly in place. "Let me go. . . ." she whispered a protest. But her words were stopped as his lips closed over hers. This time there was no gentleness about him as his body demanded a response from hers. She tried to close her own lips in a firm line of defense, but he would have none of it. Savagely he assaulted her mouth, until—involuntarily—she found herself opening to the skillful mastery of his lips and tongue. Feeling her weakness, he pressed the attack. One hand left her shoulder to travel languidly down her back, leaving a trail of heightened sensation in its wake. At the same time he pressed her slender body against the hard length of his own and deepened the kiss with an unhurried intensity. When his lips left hers to graze the line of her jaw and nuzzle her sensitive earlobe, Rachel was momentarily lost to conscious thought. The maddening touch of his warm mouth on her skin, the firm muscles of his torso and legs—all the masculinity of his presence that she had tried to ignore earlier had full possession of her senses now. She was so completely mastered that, when his hand touched the front of her blouse, she found herself instinctively leaning slightly away from him to provide better access to her breasts.

Jason did not ignore the unconscious invitation. Swiftly he slipped open the top button and leaned down to kiss lightly the curve of her breast where it swelled just above the line of her lacy white bra.

"See, you really did miss me," he murmured, his voice edged with teasing irony.

Rachel's body stiffened, and her face reddened with mortification. At the same time the sound of waiting students rustling around outside her door penetrated her swirling confusion like a surgeon's knife. Suddenly a vivid recollection of her humiliation in Jonathan's office leaped into her mind—in lurid colors. It was happening again. Convulsively she pushed Jason away and fumbled to refasten her top button.

"Get your hands off me," she hissed. "I won't be made a fool of in an office again."

Jason's dark eyebrows writhed upward in surprise. "In an office *again*?" he repeated, underlining the last word. And then his eyes took on a sharp gleam. "Do you have me confused with someone else, Ms. Pritchard? This is the first time I remember kissing you in your office."

Rachel's cheeks flamed anew. She *was* confusing this moment with the past incident. But she certainly wasn't going to admit that. "You get out of here right now," she demanded.

Jason stood surveying her expression of defiance for a moment, his gaze roaming speculatively over her flushed cheeks and overbright eyes. And then, without another word, he turned and left the room, closing the door very carefully behind him.

Mercifully a few minutes of his conference time still remained. And somehow she was able to pull herself together before the next student, a Ms. Collins, tapped on the door. Rachel looked carefully into the girl's face when she entered, trying to discern any sign that the students in the anteroom were aware of what had just transpired behind her door. But Ms. Collins and the others who followed her seemed blissfully unaware of the stormy scene between their teacher and Jason Brand.

CHAPTER FIVE

Following the episode in her office with Jason Brand, Rachel was barely able to go through the motions of seeing her other students for conferences. The remainder of the workday passed in a blur. And after driving home like a robot on automatic pilot, she threw together a dinner and then only picked at it distractedly.

"Somehow I'm going to have to settle down and get some work done," she murmured, her troubled eyes lifting from the lukewarm cup of herbal tea in her hands and gazing apprehensively at the tumbled pile of student notebooks now scattered over her slatted wood coffee table. From across the room it was impossible to pick out which was Jason Brand's; it was mixed unobtrusively with the others. But she knew it was there, waiting for her. The thought was almost as intimidating as having the man himself here with her, she thought, shivering slightly as she remembered again the vivid details of what had happened in her office that afternoon. Jason Brand had the power to kindle strong emotions in her, not just through his physical presence but also through his writing. He had proved that quite well with his last journal entry.

What had he written this time? Instinctively she knew it would be different from the last one. But she also knew it wasn't going to be ordinary.

Sighing and turning away, Rachel went into the kitchen to wash the dishes. Anything to put off the moment when she would have to open Jason Brand's latest baiting communication. But all the time she was rinsing dishes, wiping off the counter, and scouring the frying pan, her thoughts were focused on the man. Twice now, when she had been alone with Jason Brand, she had fallen under his spell. Each time she had thought she could handle him—and had been mistaken.

But he's not even here now, she told herself sternly, setting her lips in a firm line. Surely you can deal with whatever he's written this time. It's not going to take you by surprise, after all. So stop behaving like a trembling maiden about to be assaulted.

The advice made sense. Throwing her dish towel down on the counter, Rachel turned and marched back into the living room. Shuffling quickly through the pile of notebooks on the coffee table, she located Jason Brand's and set it resolutely on top. But the familiar name scrawled boldly in black across the cover seemed to her a mocking challenge.

You've really worked yourself up into a state over this, haven't you, Rachel chided herself. You've got to calm down. Turning back to the kitchen, she opened a lower cabinet and pulled out a bottle of sherry. Only on rare occasions did she drink anything alcoholic, so her expression was rueful as she carried the glass of honey-colored wine back to the couch. Kicking off her shoes, she curled up among the loose pillows strewn there. Relax, she told herself, taking a small sip of the warming liquid and then another. Staring off into space, she rolled the small glass between her hands, letting the wine help her unwind. In a few minutes she felt calm enough to put the empty glass down and reach for the journal.

Settling down into her nest of pillows, she held the thin notebook on her lap for a moment. *Why do I still feel like Pandora about to take the lid off the forbidden box?* she wondered. And then with a resolute flip of her wrist, she opened the cover.

Dear Journal,

Ms. Pritchard advised that we use these notebooks as forums for expressing thoughts and ideas. Well, since she's what's on my mind and—for some reason I've yet to fathom—she's closed off other avenues of communication, I'm going to write my thoughts and ideas about her.

Three days a week I am the lovely Ms. Pritchard's most attentive student. However, the reason my attention is riveted to her in class has nothing to do with punctuation, paragraph construction, or the organization of an essay. Though I'm sure every word she's uttered on these subjects is golden, the truth is, I haven't heard any of it. My mind has been much too preoccupied with other concerns. It's been busy admiring the color and texture of her hair, the way her lashes sometimes shadow her cheek, and the long, lissome line of her calves beneath her formidably sensible hemlines.

And then there's the softness of her mouth and the

even more tantalizing softness where the buttons of her blouse strain when she moves in certain devastating little ways.

Rachel lifted her gaze from the page, her eyes unfocused and her mind turned inward. She was thinking of her own intense physical awareness of Jason Brand's body whenever they were in the same room together. She'd tried so hard to ignore him. But she was always so acutely conscious of the ripple of strong muscles under his knit pullovers when he shifted in his seat; the tight fit of his jeans; the blue of his eyes, which could change so quickly from warm azure to storm-dark pools. His mouth, too, was so changeable, she reflected. She could remember its softness as his lips had gently urged hers apart that night after the lecture. But it could be hard and demanding, too, like in her office this afternoon. And what about the touch of his strong hands on her overheated skin, making her melt against the leanness of his body. . . . With a start Rachel realized in which direction her mind had wandered. Cut it out, she scolded herself. What's wrong with you?

She knew it was dangerous to read on. But like an unwary swimmer sucked into a whirlpool, she was powerless to resist its pull.

How often have I imagined myself divesting Ms. Pritchard of her prim little shirts—undoing the buttons one by one while I look into those cool gray eyes and watch them kindle as they read the purpose in mine. But my imagination never stops there. Since I'm a storyteller at heart, I must add the right setting, costumes, and dialogues to these little mental exercises of mine.

Would Ms. Pritchard be surprised or shocked to know that while she's lecturing on comma splices, my mind is miles away? I'm picturing her marooned on a desert island with me—or playing Jane to my Tarzan. Would her hand hesitate while she's diagraming sentences on the blackboard if she knew I was mentally abducting her from a castle or forcing her onto my pirate ship where, under threat of walking the plank unless she does my wicked will, she offers herself to me with only a token struggle to make her inevitable submission more interesting? (Note: I would, of course, never really throw her delightful body to the sharks. I want it too much for myself.)

Dear Journal, perhaps you're puzzled or confused by all this. To give you a better idea what I'm manufacturing in my overheated brain, let me describe one of my scenarios in detail. It takes place in a Middle Eastern slave market where my poor Ms. Pritchard is being cruelly auctioned off to the highest bidder. I, of course, happen along at the last moment to save her from a fate worse than death—that is, winding up in a bed other than mine!

Rachel sat very still, her fingers gripping the notebook with viselike intensity. For a moment the words on the page blurred together, and her mind spun, carrying her away from this prosaic room and into the very scene that Jason Brand was describing. Then her vision cleared, and she read quickly on.

Though all the other girls lined up for sale are seminude in filmy costumes, my Rachel is unaccountably garbed in full Freshman Composition–teacher

83

regalia. Her sexless long-sleeved blouse is spotless, and her familiar khaki skirt is crisp. Even her red hair is pulled back tightly. But the males, who are gathered around the platform where the auctioneer is pointing out the attractions of her body, are not fooled by this disguise. Neither am I. Days spent in class speculating about what that outfit conceals have whetted my curiosity to the screaming point.

As she cowers away from the crowd's probing eyes, looking pitiful, terrified, and achingly desirable, bids become frantic. Eastern potentates dripping with jewels vie for the opportunity to own the proud beauty. But none is more determined to take her home than I, and the others are outbid. As the sun sets I triumphantly lead Ms. Pritchard through the market and out on the desert to my tent. When I throw her across the silken coverlet of my pillow-strewn bed, she only glares at me in her usual defiance. But now I have all the time in the world to break down her resistance.

It was a scene Rachel could imagine well, not only because of the way Jason Brand had painted it, but also through her own remembered encounters with him. He had tried to break down her resistance before, and she had almost yielded. She could feel again his sun-browned hand burning through the thin material of her Oriental robe. He had pressed her pliant body against the whipcord leanness of his. And for a moment she had molded herself against his narrow hips and opened her mouth to the exquisite demand of his kiss.

Now her hands shook as she imagined how the scene he was describing would end. There would be no escape from

84

his tent. He would slowly take off her clothes, pausing often to kiss and caress her skin. Her body would come alive under his hands and lips. Her breasts would tauten toward him, and her mouth would open at his practiced exploration. She would arch her body eagerly against his. And then she would melt under his touch like a piece of Turkish taffy left too long in strong sunlight.

Rachel threw the journal down with an explosive gasp and covered her hot face with her hands. She knew without looking in a mirror that she was almost the color of a ripe tomato. A tide of feverish blood was flowing riotously under her skin.

"The man's a—a devil," she muttered incoherently. What's he trying to do to me? But she already knew the answer to that. It was perfectly obvious what he was trying to do. And what was even more alarming, he was succeeding. The images he had conjured up were flickering before her mind's eye like a torrid Hollywood extravaganza. And how perfectly he had cast himself, she mused, as she pictured his commanding form in the flowing garments of a desert sheikh, his eyes blue and burning behind their thick barrier of black lashes.

Convulsively she pushed her hands away from her flushed face and let them drop to her lap. But there they came once more in contact with the journal, which seemed to sear through the materials of her skirt as though its paper had been set aflame. Her own overheated imagination, she realized, was leaping up to match his—which, of course, was exactly what he'd intended. *Well, I won't play into his hands,* she told herself fiercely. *I will not look at any more of it.* But even as she formed the denial in her mind, her traitorous eyes were dropping back to the thick slanting strokes filling the page her finger now touched.

The journal continued with the indefatigable cheer of a naughty schoolboy:

> Though most of the fantasies I have about Ms. Pritchard are mentally acted out in her class, there's one that's a little different. In this little reverie I become an invisible man and follow her home.
>
> Imagine my suppressed joy as I slip into her car while she, completely unawares, starts up her motor and heads out of the parking lot. Perhaps I yield to temptation and let my breath feather the back of her neck. I might even whisper an endearment into the tender shell of her ear; and she looks around, startled, thinking she's imagining things. But if I'm wise, I control my desires for the moment and am silent. After all, I don't want to alarm my lovely instructor while she's driving. Later, when we're alone together in her apartment, will be time enough to set her pulse racing.
>
> But once I've followed Ms. Pritchard through her door, I can think seriously about how and when I will first touch my scholarly beauty. Will I take her in my arms at once? Or will I wait, playing the hunter to let my tension build while she eats her dinner and settles down for a dull evening of paper-grading?

Rachel's head snapped up; and she gazed around her empty, darkened living room with startled eyes. How had he guessed so accurately what her evenings were like? It was uncanny! Her gaze sought out the far corners while a superstitious shiver trembled down her spine. What if he actually was there in the room with her? And then a smoldering anger began to replace the alarm in her expression. Jason Brand had probably known she'd react like a fool to these words. She could just imagine his unbridled glee if he could see her peering around her living room, waiting for an invisible man to jump out of the shadows.

Her mouth compressed in a straight line, and she dropped her head to finish reading. The journal went on matter-of-factly:

> I think the best strategy is to wait until bedtime. Ms. Pritchard looks to me like the type who enjoys a warm shower before retiring. Tonight she's going to enjoy it a lot more than she expected.

Unconsciously Rachel's mouth dropped open. How had he known about her bathing habits? It was downright eerie.

> Since I'm squeamish about cold showers, I'll wait before I join her. In the meantime I don't expect to be bored, since I'll have had the pleasure of watching her disrobe. What do you think? Will she be surprised when an invisible lover begins to scrub her back? Will she appreciate my efforts when I tenderly wash for her all those out-of-the-way hard-to-reach places? Oh, I intend to be better than a rubber ducky in Ms. Pritchard's bath. She hasn't yet begun to imagine the washtime delights I plan for her. I shall kiss and caress her lovely wet flesh until it's squeaky clean. And then, after I dry her off, I intend to carry her into the bedroom, where I will be the teacher in a bedtime ritual guaranteed to delight us both. I will be a very fine invisible lover—so fine that it won't be long

before she's begging to see me in the flesh. But I think I'll make her wait. After all, hasn't she made me wait until I'm sick with repressed desire?

In the beginning I would have courted Ms. Pritchard with all the decorum she could have wished. I would have taken her out to dinner and the theater, engaged in long conversations about the state of the arts and education, and in short played the proper suitor. But cruel Ms. Pritchard has cut off the conventional routes to winning her favor and forced me to work out my longings in daydreams. Still, I'm not yet totally discouraged. Rachel, I'm a man who doesn't give up easily, and over the years my dreams have had a way of becoming reality.

Thoroughly shaken, Rachel sat staring down at the page for a long time. It was without a doubt the most incredible journal she had ever read, and she was totally staggered by it. Why had he written such a thing to her? What did he imagine her reaction would be? And, more to the point, what was her reaction?

Well, part of it at least would have been obvious even to an onlooker. She was trembling. Rachel would have got up to get herself more wine except that her legs felt like limp spaghetti, and she wasn't sure she'd be able to hold the glass without spilling it.

Another part of her reaction was confusing even to herself. She felt as though she had been emotionally overcharged. The blood racing excitedly through her veins was fueled partly by anger and mortification, partly by pleasure and amusement, and partly by—yes, she had to admit it—sexual arousal. *If Jason Brand walked through that door right now and took me in his arms,* she conceded, *I would probably turn into the abandoned woman panting for his touch that he described.*

The admission was humiliating and frightening. She had never felt so vulnerable and hunted before in her life. Even when she'd made a fool of herself over Jonathan, she'd somehow been able to think it was all an unlucky misunderstanding that had caught her unawares. But there was no pretending to misunderstand Jason. He was being as plain as day. He wanted her, and despite her resolve to keep him at arm's length he was pursuing her with the single-minded determination of a hungry tiger who'd scented fresh game.

Rachel had thought to use the teacher-student relationship as an excuse to put him off, but he had just made a joke of that defense. There was no way she could lecture in a cool and dignified manner with those mocking blue eyes caressing her. In fact, how was she going to deal with him in class at all? The thought of confronting him in a room full of students, while she knew all the time what was going on in his mind, made her want to run and hide. He'd said he was good at knocking down walls, and he'd just proved it.

Pushing the journal onto the floor, Rachel got to her feet and began pacing distractedly around the room. What was she going to do? She was seriously alarmed now, as much by her own feelings as by Jason himself. *If I let this go on any longer, he'll have me in his bed or reduced to total incoherence in the classroom,* Rachel acknowledged bitterly. *And either way,* she added, *I'll be the loser. Starting an affair with a man like him would be crazy from just about every point of view imaginable. I couldn't handle it either professionally or emotionally.* Rachel's mouth compressed in defense. There was just no way around it. Somehow she was going to have the writer taken out of her class.

"Even," she muttered aloud, "if it means going to Charles Riddle tomorrow on my knees, I'm going to get Jason Brand removed from my class."

Having made that decision, Rachel paced aimlessly around for a few more minutes and then, sighing, moved toward her bedroom. She was far too exhausted and over-wrought to do any more work tonight. Perhaps a warm shower would relax some of her tension and allow her to get a decent night of sleep so that she'd be able to face the ordeal she'd set herself for the morning.

A few minutes later Rachel adjusted the taps in her small blue-tiled bathroom and then automatically shed her clothes to step into the steamy waterfall. Rubbing a bar of soap between her hands to work up a lather, Rachel exhaled a soft sigh of pleasure as she breathed in the steam from the spray and slowly revolved, feeling the silken slide of the falling drops against her flesh. For a long time she simply stood still in the watery enclosure, delighting in the myriad sensations of warmth and wetness and letting her muscles relax.

Much of her tension seemed gradually to drain away with the water. But as she began to soap her naked breasts, she suddenly stiffened with alarm once again. All at once, Rachel could imagine she felt the touch of hard male hands stroking the sensitive skin on her back in languor-ous motions; she could almost sense the presence of a lean male body pressed close to hers. It was an illusion, of course, the product of an overstimulated imagination. But the thought was sending shivers down her spine, making her breasts feel strangely heavy, and starting up a long unfamiliar ache deep inside her.

CHAPTER SIX

Rachel spent a great part of the next morning nerving herself to approach Charles Riddle about removing Jason Brand from her class. But, much to her surprise, when she stopped by her mailbox after her last class, she discovered a phone message summoning her to the department chairman's office.

What could he want? she asked herself, nervously turning the slip of paper over in her hand. Had Brand got to him first? Was she in trouble? Unconsciously chewing on her lower lip, Rachel headed uncertainly down the polished asphalt tile corridor that led to Charles Riddle's comfortably appointed quarters. This is ridiculous, she told herself, and her lips curled wryly at her own foolishness. She hadn't done anything wrong, so why should she be so worried? It was Jason Brand who was the troublemaker, and she was going to make that fact clear to Charles Riddle.

Nevertheless, Rachel was prepared for an unreceptive

hearing. She had started off on the wrong foot with Riddle her first semester at Quincy Adams when she had rejected his amorous advances. The department chairman had been at first astonished and then insulted. This semester he had gone out of his way to treat her with the kind of frigid correctness that made it difficult to speak of even trivial matters. So Rachel was totally thrown by his friendly reception that afternoon.

Her mind prepared for a cold welcome, Rachel was astonished by the genial smile filling Charles Riddle's floridly handsome face. She found the silver-haired departmental sovereign lounging in his leather-padded easy chair, his polished Givenchy Oxford-clad feet cradled in a half-open desk drawer. A handmade silk shirt was open at the throat beneath the V neck of a tan cashmere pullover.

Tapping a pipe against an ashtray, he took in Rachel's uncertain air with a widening smile. In reaction she found herself smoothing out her gray flannel skirt and pulling back her shoulders.

"Sit down, my dear girl," he directed in his most practiced lord-of-the-manor voice, sweeping a hand grandly toward one of the green leather wingback chairs facing his desk. As Rachel's knees bent obediently and she sank into the cushioned leather, Riddle eyed her with the expectant glint of a cat toying with a grounded sparrow. "I can't wait to see the expression on your pretty face when I tell you the wonderful news I've got," he purred.

Caught completely off guard, Rachel could only stare back wordlessly.

"Yes," he continued, "Jason Brand and I have struck a most agreeable bargain." At the mention of the writer's name Rachel's gray eyes narrowed, and she surveyed Riddle's self-satisfied expression guardedly. So this did have something to do with Brand.

The department chairman's next words brought everything into focus with sharply etched clarity. "As you know, the university wants to cooperate with Mr. Brand in every possible way. He's writing a book that will put us on the map, and so naturally we're anxious to see that he has everything he needs to complete his work satisfactorily. And as it turns out, one of the things he needs is a research assistant. He's made it clear that you're the perfect choice."

The announcement destroyed Rachel's composure. "Research assistant," she repeated dumbfoundedly. "You can't be serious. Why, I already have a full load of classes. How could I possibly take on anything else?"

But Riddle only favored her with a fulsome smile and brought his fingertips together in a complacent arch. "Oh, that's all taken care of," he countered smoothly. "I've already arranged for someone to take over your classes. You can be off the university payroll and onto Mr. Brand's by tomorrow."

While she struggled to absorb that piece of information, Riddle shot her a look of such smug satisfaction that Rachel had to grab the arms of her chair to keep from leaping up and marching out of the room.

"The semester is half over. Surely you can't think this would be fair to my students."

Riddle's false smile only hardened into concrete. "Your students will be quite adequately taken care of. You need have no qualms about that."

How dare he behave in such a high-handed manner, Rachel told herself. Why, she could sue the university for breach of contract. Just wait until the faculty grievance committee hears about this! Rachel thought.

"My contract—" she began to clip out coldly.

"Might not have been renewed next semester," he completed the sentence for her helpfully. "We do have a policy of reviewing critically the continued appointment of staff members who aren't working toward the Ph.D." Rachel's mouth fell open; lost for words, she found herself staring at Riddle. "But we could consider this important assignment with Jason Brand as a sign of your interest in furthering your development as a scholar," he added pointedly.

"My development as a scholar," Rachel repeated in open disbelief. They both knew perfectly well that this assignment had nothing at all to do with her scholarly abilities. And she could see from the smirk on Riddle's face that he was enjoying this knowledge to the fullest. Seeing her backed into a corner was obviously giving him a lot of pleasure.

"I know this plum is bound to cause some jealousy among your colleagues," he continued silkily, "but if you'll put yourself completely in my hands, I have the influence to keep any envious murmurings at a minimum."

Envious murmurings! Oh, she could just imagine what form those would take. The nerve of the man! He was making a travesty of this interview. Well, she wouldn't stand for it!

"Doctor Riddle," she began determinedly, "why was I not consulted before you went ahead and found a replacement for me?"

But Riddle held up his hand. "Ms. Pritchard, the university's reputation is at issue here. Surely you can see the need for expediency in this matter." He gave her an appraising look. "I suppose, if you wanted to make trouble for yourself, you could complain to the faculty grievance committee. But you must realize how foolish that would be. You're being offered an opportunity that most young scholars with your limited background would jump at."

Rachel had to force herself to breathe evenly. She felt trapped. She supposed that from Riddle's point of view this really did seem like an opportunity. In fact, most people would see it that way. But then most people knew nothing of her previous experience as a research assistant —and she wanted to keep it that way. If she made trouble over this, would the department chairman start digging around in her background to find some other weapon he could use against her? The thought was mortifying. But maybe there was something she could do to protect herself at least partially.

With all the composure she could muster Rachel asked, "How would it look on my record if I just quit in the middle of the semester? I couldn't accept this post without a letter from you nominating me for it."

Riddle looked momentarily disconcerted. Clearly he hadn't expected her to think of that. And Rachel got a certain ironic pleasure in seeing the shift of expressions on his face.

"Very well, I'll see that there's a letter," he conceded tightly. "Now, is that the end of your objections?"

What more could she say?

"This has been very sudden, and I'll have to give it some thought," Rachel hedged, rising stiffly to her feet.

Riddle had won and they both knew it. "Certainly," he agreed with false graciousness. "But let me know your decision by the end of the day."

As she retraced her path and went back to her office, Rachel's thoughts were in turmoil. In desperate need of someone to talk with she was relieved to find Marta's door open. Her inner distress must have been mirrored in her face, for when Marta looked up from the inevitable stack of papers littering her desk, her expression became concerned.

"What's wrong?" she exclaimed. "You look as if you're about to come apart at the seams. Did one of your students just threaten assault with a deadly weapon?"

Rachel could only manage the ghost of a smile. She did feel as though she had been assaulted. "No student," she explained. "It was our department chairman. I've just been replaced." And then, in response to Marta's shocked look, she hastily recounted the whole crazy interview. But when she finished, Marta's reaction was not the one she expected.

"Listen, I can't defend the way things were done," the other young woman pointed out, "but it really is an opportunity. I'd give anything to get away from all these papers for a while. And, for heaven's sake, Rachel, think about what it's going to do for your résumé. Having helped Jason Brand write one of his best sellers is going to sound darn glamorous. You might even be able to get an article out of it for the *Harper's.*"

Rachel stared at her friend helplessly. It was obvious that without all the facts nobody was going to see this from her point of view. And there was no way she was going to give even Marta all the facts about either her experiences at Winthrop or the various sensual assaults Jason Brand had been making on her defenses lately.

Sighing, Rachel sat down in the metal folding chair adjacent to Marta's. She would have to say *something* to justify her point of view. "I haven't told anyone," she admitted in a smothered voice. "Jason Brand has been coming on to me pretty strong lately, and I just don't know if I can handle him."

Marta cocked her head and laughed. "So that's what been bothering you. I wondered. But I must say, the two of you look as if you'd go together like ice cream and hot fudge sauce." Marta grinned impishly. "And even though I'm on a diet, I still think that's a dynamite combination."

Rachel shot her friend a disbelieving look. But Marta only laughed. "Why don't you make it work *for* you instead of against you? After all, that's what women have been doing since Eve first offered Adam the apple. Let Brand know it has to be a professional relationship—and then exploit the situation for all it's worth. Doing any kind of research on his book has got to make fending off a few passes worth the effort."

Rachel looked up uncertainly. "You really think I could pull that off?" she asked with a crooked smile.

Marta gave her a grin. "I've never seen the man you couldn't handle, Rachel. Remember how you made that Hemingway scholar on sabbatical from L.S.U. back off last semester?"

Rachel had to laugh. Sitting here in Marta's cozy office, it was easy to believe she could deal with Jason Brand. What other tricks could he try now? She knew them all, and that gave her the upper hand. She would keep up her defenses, she told herself. And when he saw her new determination, he would surely back off. For the first time in hours Rachel felt relaxed enough to be able to think of something besides her own problems.

"Hey, what a clod I am! I've been so busy talking about

myself, I didn't even notice what you've done to your hair."

Marta patted her new permanent and moved her head from side to side. "Do you like it?" she asked hesitantly. When Rachel nodded with enthusiasm, her colleague stood up and did a pirouette. "And I've lost six pounds too. What do you think about that?"

"I think it's great," Rachel said, smiling. "And I suspect I won't even recognize you a few weeks from now."

Marta sat back down, beaming from ear to ear. "That's what I'm hoping, too, and not just because I intend to stick with my diet," she agreed, gesturing at a pile of glossy fashion magazines forming a small mountain at the corner of her desk. "I've been reading these all weekend to pick up tips. It's just like researching a master's thesis or a long paper, only now I'm using my brains to see if I can't do something with myself instead of my career."

The two women chatted for a few more minutes, and then Rachel returned to her office feeling much calmer. *I might as well call Riddle's secretary right now and tell her I've accepted the new assignment,* she told herself. *And when I've done that, I'd better see Jason Brand.*

Like everyone else in the English department, Rachel knew that the writer had been given a V.I.P. suite of the type normally reserved for distinguished visiting professors.

Standing with her hand raised to knock on the polished wood door, she wondered if she had made the right decision. Down in Marta's office it had been easy to imagine she could handle anything the writer threw at her. But now she wasn't quite so confident. Would Brand attempt to intimidate her? Would he try to force her into a compromising position? She grimaced; she was not looking forward to this interview. But it was something that had to be done. Decisively her knuckles came down on the wood surface.

"Come in," Jason Brand's deep voice rumbled through the door. Taking a deep breath, Rachel turned the knob and stepped across the threshold.

Brand was standing in front of a bookcase jammed with books and papers, apparently searching fruitlessly for something. As he raked a hand through his dark hair his face turned toward her, still wearing the impatient expression of a man who can't find what he wants. His look changed, though, when he saw Rachel; and his well-formed features molded themselves into a smile of welcome.

"To what do I owe the honor?" he inquired.

Rachel felt a defensive surge of irritation. But she refused to play games with him over this.

"You know perfectly well why I'm here," she shot back. "I'm here because Charles Riddle made it clear that I'd lose my job if I didn't agree to become your research assistant."

Jason frowned. "Did he really? Well, that was not my intention when I recommended you. But I'm very happy, that is, if you've decided to accept the position."

Rachel scrutinized his features with open disbelief. He was making it sound as though blackmailing her with the threat of losing her job were all Riddle's idea. But Jason Brand was not soft-soaping her into believing a word of that. "You don't fool me," she told him bitingly. "I don't trust you an inch, and you might as well know it right now."

Jason's face darkened, and he opened his mouth to say

something. But Rachel was wound up now and hurried on before he could speak. "I want you to know that research is all I'm going to do for you. So if you expect—"

"Now, just a second, Ms. Pritchard," he injected forcefully. "I requested you strictly because of your professional qualifications. I expect you to work closely with me on my book and to do a good job. Nothing extracurricular is required, so you can relax on that score." He gestured at the bookcase. "You can start by finding the Quincy Adams catalogue. I thought it was here, but if it is, I've hidden it so thoroughly that I can't make it surface."

As he spoke he turned back to his desk and began to shuffle through a stack of student questionnaires. Rachel, lost for words, stared at his tall form. Did he really expect her to believe that little speech? He'd been trying to get to her all semester, and this could only be a new tack in his campaign.

But if that's what it was, Jason Brand hid his intentions well. For the next few days he was the perfect boss—businesslike, polite, and considerate. He even gave Rachel time off to say good-bye to her students, and she took advantage of the opportunity to say a special farewell over lunch at the student cafeteria to Ms. Sachs and encouraged her to continue with her writing. When Rachel went back to her new office later that day, she wondered what the future held for her too. But the crisp professional facade Jason Brand had assumed gave her no clue as yet.

CHAPTER SEVEN

Three weeks later Rachel was working alone in the new office she was sharing with Jason Brand when the phone rang. She had been reviewing index-card notes from an interview, and her mind was still on the revealing nature of the remarks she had been scanning as she picked up the receiver.

"So do you still hate the job, stranger?" a laughing voice inquired. The faint frown creasing Rachel's brow smoothed out, and a smile curved her lips. The voice on the other end of the line was Marta's.

"Hi, Marta. I was planning on calling you today."

"Oh, really?" the disembodied voice teased. "Well, I was wondering what had happened to you. I haven't seen you for days and I was beginning to fear that big, bad Jason Brand had swallowed you whole."

Rachel shrugged helplessly as she reassured her friend otherwise. But it was true: She hadn't been available much lately.

"Jason working you pretty hard?" Marta queried.

"A regular Simon Legree." But at the same time Rachel had to concede she was finding it exciting to work for someone with the confidence, experience, and drive of Jason Brand. It was exhilarating and fascinating to conduct the interviews and research that were to form the foundation for his study. Already she was beginning to see the manuscript take shape, and she was excited about it. There was something deeply satisfying about being in on the making of what, Rachel was now convinced, would be a very influential and significant work.

Though she had fought against taking the job as his research assistant and resented the overbearing way he'd used Riddle to rope her in, she now had almost no regrets. For someone who had hopes of being a professional writer herself, it was the chance of a lifetime—and she knew it. Maybe Jason Brand's motives in offering her the post were suspect, but that was a separate issue.

When Rachel had first started the new assignment, she had circled around Jason Brand like a wary cat, ready to jump if he made the slightest move that could be construed as a pass. But his behavior during the three weeks she had been in his employ had been exemplary. Gone was the macho seducer she'd tried unsuccessfully to cope with earlier. Instead, he was witty, charming, even courtly in his demeanor. And gradually Rachel had begun to respond, relaxing her guard and allowing herself by degrees to enjoy his company more than she knew was wise.

After making plans with Marta to meet for lunch, Rachel put down the receiver thoughtfully. It was as though, she mused, brushing a strand of hair off her forehead, he had decided to change his tactics toward her. When, in her role of teacher, she had made herself unavailable, her aloofness had seemed to bring out the implacable hunter in him. And he had become increasingly aggressive in his attempts to force her acknowledgment of the sexual attraction between them.

Now that he had got her into his power and they were working closely together on a daily basis, he had become softer. Yet, behind all that persuasive charm, Rachel sensed that Jason's original purpose hadn't changed. For the time being, he was on good behavior; allowing her to fall under the spell of his considerable appeal. But sooner or later he would tire of the waiting game and make his move. Would she succumb to it? Rachel asked herself ruefully. Part of her answered, *No, not if I have a brain in my head.* But part of her had begun to contemplate the prospect with a delicious sense of anticipation. The realization brought her up short, and she took a shuddering breath as she recognized it for the dangerous weakness it was. If she relaxed her guard, Jason was going to get to her, and in the long run it would just be another emotional disaster she couldn't cope with.

Rachel squared her shoulders and stiffened her spine. "Well, he's not going to," she said under her breath. "This relationship is going to be strictly business, nothing more. I'm going to walk away from it with my self-respect intact."

It was this determination she repeated to Marta later that day over a cottage cheese–and–fruit salad.

"I'm not in love with Mr. Brand, and I'm not about to make an idiot of myself over him," she exclaimed in reply to her friend's probing questions. And then, taking in Marta's skeptical look, Rachel hurriedly changed the subject. "Let's talk about you, Marta. I just can't get over the changes I can see already. You're a new woman!"

It was true. It seemed to Rachel that Marta was like a butterfly wriggling free of an imprisoning chrysalis. In the past three weeks she'd shed ten more pounds and taken a course in makeup. With her trimmer figure and the wreath of soft curls now framing her subtly colored features, the transformation was startling.

Rachel put down her fork and leaned back to study her friend appreciatively. "You're turning into a regular Cinderella," she kidded lightly.

Surprisingly Marta blushed and then replied with uncharacteristic earnestness. "Well, if I'm Cinderella, you're my fairy godmother. You were my inspiration, Rachel. When we went shopping that day in Georgetown, I decided I was going to follow your advice—and your example."

A little embarrassed by her outburst, Marta's cheeks flushed becomingly. Rachel was embarrassed, too, but she was also deeply touched. Impulsively she leaned forward and patted her friend's hand. "I'm really flattered. But pretty soon I'm the one who's going to be following your example. You look smashing, Marta." Rachel grinned. "Say, how about celebrating our mutual admiration society by seeing a movie tonight in Georgetown? We could even go back to that place and buy some more fancy underwear. I'm a sap for silk and lace, though I haven't yet had the courage to wear that teddy I bought."

But Marta shook her head with an impish grin. "Sorry. Not tonight, Rachel. I've already got a date to see a movie."

Rachel arched an eyebrow. "Oh-ho! Anybody I know?"

Marta blushed again and then added shyly, "Yes . . . Tom Metcalf."

Rachel's eyebrows climbed even more steeply, and she slanted a sparkling look that demanded an explanation.

Laughing self-consciously, Marta held up a nicely manicured hand to forestall Rachel's question. "Don't say it! I know what you're thinking, but believe me, it's no big deal. Tom was under Muffy's spell for a while. He's probably just asked me out because she turned him down to have dinner with Charles Riddle. Muffy's switched her red-hot attentions to our revered department chairman lately, or didn't you know?"

"No, I didn't know," Rachel murmured, taking a sip of tea from her cup and glancing speculatively over its rim at the nearby table where Muffy and Riddle had just sat down. They had their heads together and looked very cozy. Was Muffy angling for a big fish like Riddle because she hadn't got anywhere with Jason? Rachel wondered. She was weak enough to feel a stab of satisfaction at the idea. Quickly her gaze went back to her friend, and Rachel finished what she had been about to say.

"I don't believe for a minute that Tom asked you out only because he couldn't get a date with that predatory blonde. You're a terrific woman, Marta. And now you're a terrific-*looking* woman. Tom would be lucky to get you, and don't you forget it."

That afternoon on her way home Rachel stopped to pick up her mail. Among the usual assortment of magazine ads and departmental communications was a small package with a Boston postmark and no return address. Had any of her old friends from graduate school managed to get something published? And why would one of them go to the trouble of tracking her down to send a copy? After the shattering incident with Jonathan, she had left Winthrop wanting to bury that part of her life in a deep dark hole—which was probably why she carried the package out to her car unopened.

As she drove home her mind went back to the conversation with Marta. Rachel had to admit that she'd been disappointed when her friend turned her down for a movie. She was restless and felt as if she needed a night out. But she was too generous not to be happy for the other woman. Marta was obviously attracted to Tom; and now that he'd finally noticed her and asked her out, it looked like there might be a romance in the offing. In a lot of ways they were ideally suited to each another, Rachel mused as she pulled up at a traffic light. Their interests were the same, and Marta's sparkling wit would offset Tom's more diffident personality.

Just before the light changed, Rachel's eyes darted curiously once again to the small package lying next to her on the passenger seat. She couldn't help wondering who had sent the book and began mentally to tick off likely possibilities, rejecting each in turn.

By the time she reached her apartment house, her brows were knit in puzzlement. A few minutes later, however, the puzzled frown she wore had deepened, pleating her normally smooth forehead with deep grooves of distress. When Rachel tore open the brown paper and removed the protective cardboard wrapper, she found a slim volume of poetry. It was adorned with an abstract jacket design in shades of blue. But she hardly saw that because she was busy taking in the author's name. It leaped out at her like an assailant. VISIONS AND REGRETS: *A Book of Poetry by Jonathan Convers*, the jacket read.

Staggered, Rachel's gray eyes stretched wide; she stared down at the volume feeling as though all the blood had suddenly frozen solid in her veins. Why in the world would Jonathan, after all this time, send her his book? Then she realized it must have just come out. Hesitantly

Rachel's hand went down to the crisp dust jacket and fingered the fresh paper. Filled with curiosity, she flipped open the cover and again froze with incredulity. On the inside page, written in the neat script she remembered so well, were the words "For Rachel, who understands why. J.C."

What was that supposed to mean? How was she supposed to understand why? She didn't understand his reasons for sending her the book at all. But when she turned the page to the table of contents, a light began to dawn. Next to one of the titles there was a penciled check mark. The poem indicated was called "The Girl with the Dark Red Hair."

It was, she discovered when she began to read it, a love poem that was both sensuous and erotic. And when she had finished it, there was no doubt in her mind that it had been written about her.

She was reading the poem again later that night when she was disturbed by a peremptory tap on her door. Laying the slim volume down open on the coffee table, she got up only to find Jason Brand once more on her doorstep.

Dressed in form-fitting blue jeans and a white fisherman's knit turtleneck pullover, he looked devastatingly masculine. "I want to talk to you," he said, his face imperturbable. "May I come in?"

Rachel looked uncomfortably down at her own faded tight-fitting jeans, which emphasized the narrowness of her waist, the slender curve of her hips and the long elegant line of her legs. She had not expected company, and she was suddenly—and uneasily—aware that she was braless underneath her soft flannel shirt and that her hair hung in a careless sweep around her shoulders.

Jason Brand's blue eyes were busy taking in her appearance too. "You look fine," he drawled in his deep voice, as though reading her mind. "In fact, I like you a lot better in that outfit than in your business clothes." He grinned, his eyes twinkling with mischief. "But then you already know that, don't you."

Chuckling deep in his throat, he pushed forward so that she had to step back, reluctantly allowing him to enter. Seeing him in her living room brought back a vivid recollection of his other visit, and she felt herself begin to redden at the memory. But Jason Brand showed no sign of embarrassment. He was standing in the middle of the room with his hands in his pockets, looking idly around at her furniture as though he were about to buy the place.

"What is it you wanted to talk to me about?" she asked, shutting the door and coming forward.

"The research trips I mentioned before," he answered succinctly, moving toward the couch and sitting down on it without being invited. "I'm planning several, and I want to consult with you about them."

Rachel began to frown. "Research trips?" What did he mean by that? Surely he wasn't going to ask her to travel with him. Horrified by the possibilities that was conjuring up, she began a heated protest.

But Jason cut her short with a slicing wave of his hand. Then, stretching out his long legs and leaning his dark head against the back of the sofa as though he planned to spend the rest of the evening there, he pronounced, "Of course, you'll come with me. I intend to interview intensively on these trips, and having you there will mean I can get twice as much done."

He lifted his head and gave her a challenging look, amusement lurking in his blue eyes. In her consternation

Rachel had perched uncertainly on the edge of the couch. But now something in his expression as he surveyed her made her think better of that. She began to get up, with the idea of taking a seat at a safe distance in one of her two armchairs. But Jason had divined her intention, and before she was able to scramble to her feet, his muscular hand closed around her wrist and she found herself tumbling helplessly back onto the couch much closer to the writer's lean male form than she'd been originally.

"What do you think you're doing?" she sputtered, shooting him an indignant stare.

Jason smiled lazily down into her rounded eyes. "What's wrong? Don't you think you can have a discussion sitting next to me? And," he continued, "what are your objections to accompanying me on a trip? Or can I guess? Are you afraid I'm going to try and seduce you in some sleazy campus motel, Rachel?"

Rachel's eyes were shooting angry sparks, not least because she was so treacherously aware of Jason's body. The proximity of his lean hips and broad shoulders, the arrogant masculinity of his handsome features so close to hers, were having a disruptive effect on her breathing. Still holding her wrist, he moved closer. Leaning over her, he looked into her eyes with a faint smile lifting the corner of his well-shaped mouth.

"Well, you haven't exactly given me the impression that you're a perfect gentleman, have you?" she threw out a little desperately.

The corners of Jason's eyes crinkled with amusement as he continued to survey her, his gaze drifting over her face and lingering on her mouth so that she began to feel her skin glow with embarrassed color. "Haven't I?" he murmured softly. "But haven't I been good ever since you came to work for me? I wanted you to know that your body isn't the only thing I admire about you." He smiled with devastating charm. "I'm very taken with that neat little mind of yours too. Admit it," he whispered intimately, "I've been a gentleman."

What he said was true. But now, with him leaning toward her and inflaming her senses with such riotous effect, there was no way she would admit it graciously. "It must have been a terrible effort."

Jason laughed, revealing an even row of strong white teeth. "You're right, keeping my hands off you has been a strain. And I'm not big on making life rough on myself. Life is meant to be enjoyed as much as possible, Rachel. It's time you learned that. And, by the way, you're wrong about my intentions on these research trips. I don't intend seducing you in a motel." His mouth curled wickedly. "I hope to have done it long before that."

Rachel stiffened and tried to draw back, but it was too late. Jason's eyes seemed to dilate, an engulfing darkness blotting out their blue hue, and she felt her heart quicken in dizzy reaction. And then he was pressing her gently down into the cushions, his arms around her waist and shoulders, his mouth searching relentlessly for hers.

Rachel's heart was pounding so hard in her chest that the rush of her own blood seemed to deafen her. Almost faint from excitement, she was totally unable to think and her lips opened helplessly under his. Some part of her knew she ought to protest, attempt somehow to push him away. But those warnings were lost in the overwhelming flood of other sensations claiming her. A weakness seemed to invade her, as though her bones were melting, taking all her willpower with them.

As Jason's firm mouth explored hers, she felt the press

110

of his broad chest against her breasts and with delight took in the heady scent of his skin. It smelled of soap and his citrus after-shave and felt excitingly rough against her own. Sensations of warmth and strength seemed to flow from him and enfold her in a hypnotic fixation underlined by the heavy throb of his heart against her breasts. She moaned with half pleasure, half protest as she felt the thrust of Jason's tongue probing the moist recesses of her mouth. At the same time one of his hands began its own investigation. Sensuously his fingers stroked the fiery thickness of her hair and then moved down to fondle the soft flesh of her shoulders before sliding silkily along her arms and then possessively closing around her breast.

"Oh, God, Rachel, you don't have a bra on," he groaned, his mouth leaving hers to nibble delicately at the sensitive cords on either side of her neck. Dexterously his long fingers began to stroke and manipulate first one breast and then the other and she was helpless to stop the flood of erotic sensations that washed over her. Her nipples hardened under his knowing fingers, sending delicious darts of pleasure downward through her body. Convulsively her arms folded themselves around the broad structure of his back, feeling its flexed muscle and hard bone. And she pressed her aching body closer to his, feeling an urgency in response to his exciting masculinity. Jason's lips moved to the hollow of her throat and then tracked a path of fire downward to the V between her full breasts, while her own fingers twisted with desire in the vibrant thickness of his hair.

With growing anticipation she felt him free the buttons on her shirt. As the material fell away his mouth closed over her taut nipple, and his silky tongue licked an insistent path around it. And as his mouth moved across her

111

skin Rachel felt herself quivering, her hips thrust up against his, her own legs seeming to melt against his hard, lean thighs.

Then, shockingly, she felt the snaps of her jeans give way. Jason's hand unzippered the closure and pushed into the soft material. The feel of his long fingers sliding beneath the protective layer of her silk bikini panties jarred Rachel out of her sensual stupor. This was all happening so fast. Before she knew it, they would be making love, and though her body was aching for it, she knew she would hate herself afterward. In protest, she began to wriggle and push at his demanding hands.

"No, Jason, stop," she moaned. "We can't do this."

"Why not?" he muttered thickly, lifting his head from her breast where she could see the hard flush that lay along his high cheekbones. "We both want this. Rachel, don't stop me."

But, given a moment to come to her senses once more, Rachel's objections grew more vehement. "How can I work for you?" she began desperately.

But Jason hardly seemed to hear. "Our working relationship will be even better if we're lovers, and our research trips will be a hell of a lot more fun," he muttered, his lips sliding seductively down to the taut muscles of her bared stomach, just grazing the white flesh exposed there.

With a monumental effort of will Rachel pushed at his head and managed to slide away from him so that her upper body fell half off the couch.

His dark head reared again and he glared at her. "Rachel, for God's sake—"

"Don't Rachel me! I am not letting you make love to me, Jason Brand," she countered, her tone bordering on hysteria.

He stared at her fixedly, and she was painfully conscious of how she must look—her hair hanging in disarray and her shirt open, her breasts exposed. But her adrenaline was flowing now, and she refused to back down. The angry sparkle in her eyes and the bright spots of color in her cheeks signaled as much. Hurriedly she drew the edges of the flannel shirt together to cover her nakedness and began fumbling to button them.

Sighing with frustration, Jason reached out and pushed her shoulders unceremoniously back onto the supporting cushions and then rolled away and stood up with his back to her. She watched his shoulders heave as he took several deep, shuddering breaths and then her eyes fell away from the taut lines of his body, and she went hot all over once more with embarrassment.

What made it worse was that she knew exactly how he was feeling because she was going through the same thing herself. She had been thoroughly aroused by him, and she was aching with sexual frustration.

"I think you'd better leave," Rachel muttered, staring down at her hands.

Jason turned abruptly and gave her a hard look. "Oh, do you? Sorry to disappoint you, but I have no intention of leaving. I came here tonight to discuss my travel plans with you, and I plan on staying until I've done exactly that."

"But—but—" she stammered incoherently. Ignoring her, Jason reached down and pulled her up by the wrist.

"Go and make us each a cup of coffee, Rachel," he ordered more gently. "Maybe after we drink it, we'll both be calm enough to treat each other civilly."

His blue eyes held hers, and all her objections seemed to freeze on her tongue. She couldn't argue with him when he was like this. He was too overpowering. Turning her head away, she walked stiffly toward her small kitchen, leaving him alone in the living room.

The few minutes it took to boil water and fix mugs full of instant coffee gave Rachel a much needed chance to pull herself together. She had been subjected to a devastating sensual onslaught, and as she thought about it her temper began to rise. Jason was her employer. He had no right to subject her to this kind of sexual pressure. It was harassment.

While she put the two mugs of coffee down on a tray, she began putting together a little speech that would tell him just that. But when she carried the drinks back into the living room, something odd in the silence that hung there made her pause to lift her head like a wary animal scenting danger.

Jason was standing very still, poised in front of the coffee table with Jonathan Convers's book balanced between his sinewy brown hands. His jaw was clamped and all the lines of his tall body were taut, as though rage were coursing through it. And his eyes, Rachel noted with a terrible hollow sensation in her solar plexus, were trained with X-ray intensity on the page she had left open when she'd got up to answer his knock. He was obviously reading Jonathan's poem.

Hearing her involuntary gasp of dismay, Jason's dark head slowly lifted from the lines he was scanning and his eyes met hers with an almost physical impact. All the warmth had left his expression. His eyes were glacial, an arctic blue like reflective chunks chipped from some dangerous and long-submerged iceberg. Slowly he began to quote:

Her skin like living silk,
And the rusty flame of her hair
Winding itself through my fingers,
Clinging to my flesh in
Threads of warm desire.

The words of the poem were clipped out through his bared teeth with distaste, as though they were bitter on his tongue.

Very carefully Rachel set the tray down on an end table. The cups rattled because her hands were trembling, and as she straightened to face Jason, she could feel the blood draining from her cheeks.

Jason's eyes savaged her. "Now I know why Jonathan Convers gave you such a glowing recommendation. Oh, yes," he added bitingly, seeing her look of surprise. "I checked your references. Did you think I was fool enough to hire you just because I wanted you in my bed? No, I always insist on getting my money's worth. I made sure you could do the job. I even read the short story you thoughtfully submitted with your application. So I knew you could write as well as deliver literary criticism." Jason's voice dripped acid. "But let's get back to Jonathan Convers. According to the good professor, whose research assistant you were before me, you can definitely do the job all right. He rated your performance as A-plus." Jason closed the book with a vicious snap, as though he would like to break it in half, and then sent it skidding across the floor, where it slammed into a corner and then fell with a dull thud, its pages splayed open.

Rachel's eyes followed it with shocked disbelief. Her throat felt as though there were hot ground glass clogging it; her heart was banging against her ribs with the slow, painful swings of a cement wrecking ball.

"Now I understand that remark about being made love to in an office again. Is that where the two of you did it? My God, what a fool you've been making of me," he snarled.

"No, no, Jason, it's not like that at all," she began haltingly.

But he was far too wound up to pay attention to her stammered attempt at an explanation.

"All this time I've been circling around trying to figure a way to get your attention. How I could have been so stupid as to have been taken in by those phony 'Don't touch me' airs."

The muscle in his jaw jumping with anger, the blue eyes murderous, Jason strode quickly forward and seized Rachel by the shoulders as though he meant to shake her. "I happen to have met Convers. He's married—with kids! All this time you've been carrying on a hole-in-the-corner affair with a married man!"

And then he did shake her. Rachel felt an emotional charge coming off him like a scorching bolt of electricity. "It's not an affair," she gasped. "I haven't seen him in more than a year."

Jason's voice was filled with caustic disbelief. "What the hell is it, then? An unusually warm classroom attachment? Do you think I'm a fool? No man writes about a woman like that unless he's slept with her!"

But now it was Rachel's turn to be derisive. "Oh, really?" she flung recklessly, her gray eyes flashing. "Would you care to compare some of the steamy passages in that journal you wrote to the lines in Jonathan's poem?"

He inhaled sharply. "Jonathan, is it?" Jason's lip curled

116

in a cruel imitation of a smile. " 'For Rachel, who understands why,' " he quoted mockingly. "Well, now I understand why too. Why you've been turning me off like a tap. You've been too busy elsewhere, haven't you?"

Jason's heavy hands dropped from her shoulders, and he looked away, his teeth clenched, his eyes almost hidden by his eyelids and the thick screen of black lashes. There was a brief, strained silence. "Do you love him?"

Rachel had been staring down at the floor. But now she quickly looked up, startled. "It's not an affair, and it never was," she denied. "I haven't seen him since I left graduate school. I had no idea he was going to write that poem or send me his book."

Jason met her gaze. His eyes were a blinding dark blue, and she flinched before the piercing impact of their thrust. "You didn't answer my question," he clipped out tersely. "Do you love him?"

Rachel's tongue seemed to tie itself in confused knots. She didn't know how to answer that, or if she wanted to. Part of her would have liked to spill out the whole degrading story. She'd told no one about it since leaving Winthrop, and sometimes she felt that hiding it away was allowing it to put down unwholesome roots that a little fresh air would quickly destroy. But Jason was the last person to whom she felt like revealing her stupidity.

"Not talking?" he commented in her ear sardonically. Clipping hard fingers around her elbow, Jason forced her to the couch and sat her down. "Tell me about it, Rachel."

"It's none of your business," she muttered obstinately, giving him an angry look through her eyelashes. She refused to be intimidated this way. The man was too overbearing altogether. Who did he think he was anyway?

Jason sat down beside Rachel and surprised her by

taking her hand in his quite gently. "I'm making it my business," he said in deep tones, beginning to stroke her fingers. "I asked you if you loved him."

Rachel sighed and turned her face away. Her jaw was rigid. She could feel tears pressing at the back of her eyes and a tight constriction in her throat. Suddenly all the months of regret, the lonely nights she'd spent brooding over the past seemed to coalesce into a big dark lump of hurt that she could no longer keep inside her.

"I guess I thought I did once," she admitted finally, "but that was a long time ago. I told you. I haven't seen him since I left Boston."

Jason caught her chin between his strong fingers and forced her to turn. "Tell me," he demanded, his blue eyes compellingly steady on hers.

And suddenly she did. The emotional logjam burst, and the whole sad, ridiculous tale came pouring out of her in a heedless rush. Jason heard her out patiently. Now and then he asked a question, but mostly he just listened with a strained, quiet intensity that Rachel was too preoccupied to try and interpret.

When she had done, he rephrased his original question. "Are you still in love with him?"

"No."

Jason regarded her dryly. "Maybe not," he said with tight emphasis. "But you're still obsessed with him. And what's more, you're still blaming yourself for something that wasn't really your fault. It explains a lot, you know. It accounts for your frozen-up attitude toward men, the atmosphere of icy untouchability you give off. Oh, yes; don't try denying it," he added, cutting off her protest. "Rachel, you've built that incident in your past way out of proportion, and now you're letting it ruin an important part of your life."

Stung, she tried to deny what he had claimed. But inwardly Rachel knew that at least some of it was true. She had allowed her humiliation over Jonathan to affect her deeply.

"You were a sitting duck for the guy," Jason snapped, his eyes sparking with anger. "Universities are full of older men like Charles Riddle and your precious Jonathan Convers. They like to play ego-gratification games with beautiful young women. The teacher-student relationship is easy for an experienced man to take advantage of." Jason laughed humorlessly. "You can hardly blame them, really. When you've got a ready-made harem in your class every semester, and all of them primed to adore you, it's damn tempting to exploit the situation."

The description did not please Rachel, and she reacted defensively. It had shocked her to have Jonathan compared with Charles Riddle. Perversely she found herself defending her former teacher.

"I was not a ready-made harem girl nor a blindly adoring fool," she flashed. "I admired Jonathan because he was sensitive, intelligent, and gifted. And I believe he admired me as a woman for the same reasons. The situation just got out of hand, that's all. Neither of us meant for it to go that far. I'm as much to blame as he."

Jason gave her an acid look and then got up and stalked to the center of the room. Turning on his heel, he jammed his hands in his pockets and said scathingly, "If you believe that, you really are an idiot. He was manipulating you, Rachel, using your naive hero-worshipping to get you into bed. It's as simple as that, so don't try and dress it up. You fell for it. What's more, you're still falling for it.

Grow up! He sent you that book because he wouldn't mind getting something going with you on the side, now that you're no longer on campus to embarrass him," Jason added nastily. "Stop telling yourself fairy tales and face the truth!"

And with that, Jason strode out of the room, slamming the door behind him, so that it rattled on its hinges.

CHAPTER EIGHT

Rachel woke up the next morning dreading another confrontation with Jason. Groaning as she stumbled out of bed, she briefly considered calling in sick. But she dismissed that as cowardly. Besides, Jason would see through that deception immediately, and if she wanted to keep her self-respect, she would have to face him. However, when she arrived at the office wearing her most conservative gray tweed suit, she found that all her anxiety had been wasted. The office was empty. Instead of the encounter she had been fearing, she found only a terse note:

I'll be out of town for a few days.

J.

Underneath it was a typed list of tasks calculated to keep her busy for at least three weeks.

Sinking into her own desk chair, Rachel thoughtfully twirled the note between her index fingers. It wasn't what she had expected at all. Was Jason avoiding today's meeting? It seemed impossible. He was so in control, so sure of himself. No, what had been a devastating evening for her had probably meant nothing to him. Having failed to get what he wanted from her, he was probably getting it somewhere else.

Rachel crumpled the note, clenching her fist around it. She could just picture him with his beautiful editor Angelique in some cozy Connecticut hideaway. Rachel shifted discontentedly, trying to tell herself that she didn't care. But it wasn't true, and she knew it. In self-torture her mind began to spin out images of Jason with a sensuously beautiful woman, probably a sultry brunette. She could just picture the two of them enjoying a glass of wine together over an intimate dinner, in each other's arms in front of a roaring fire, and finally making passionate love.

Despite all her inward protests she was becoming emotionally involved with Jason Brand. These ridiculous fantasies proved it.

Why am I doing this? Rachel asked herself disgustedly. *Am I the type of masochistic woman who enjoys tormenting herself over some worthless man? The only difference is that this time it's Jason Brand, not Jonathan Convers.* Biting her lip, she forced her thoughts away from her painful imaginings and turned to the stack of work Jason had left her—*to keep my mind occupied,* Rachel told herself with grim humor.

But her progress was slow. She couldn't keep her mind from wandering, and she found herself continually glancing at her watch. The work she had enjoyed so much in Jason's company had now become almost drudgery. But she kept doggedly pushing forward, circling good quotes in student interviews and filing useful bits of information to be used in future chapters.

I'm not going to give him the satisfaction of knowing I'm so upset, I can't concentrate on my work, she told herself, shoving a freshly cut magazine article in a manila folder.

But after three days of this toil, Rachel badly needed a break. She decided to phone and see if Marta was free for lunch.

"You're welcome to join me and Tom," her friend offered.

Rachel tried to refuse considerately, but Marta was cheerfully insistent.

At noon the three of them met at the faculty dining room. Though Rachel walked in feeling very much a fifth wheel, Tom and Marta's cheerful gossip put her at ease. And when they described the latest in the liaison between Muffy and Riddle, she found herself laughing out loud. Tom and Marta seemed to be having such a good time together that it lifted Rachel's spirits to be with them. And she couldn't help being pleased at the new turn her friend's life had taken.

Returning to the office an hour later, Rachel was feeling better than she had all week and was actually ready to tackle more of the interview forms stacked on her desk. But when she opened the door and found Jason Brand lounging at his desk, all thoughts of interview forms were instantly wiped away.

"I see you've managed to get quite a lot done in my absence," he commented, shooting her an imperturbable smile, as if nothing out of the ordinary had happened between them before his sudden trip. "And it's a good thing, because you're going to have a lot more forms to go through after our research trip to Boston tomorrow."

Rachel's eyebrows shot up. "Boston?" she exclaimed. "What are you talking about?"

"About the trip I've been away arranging," Jason explained with exaggerated patience. "Aren't you pleased to hear that our first research trip is set at your alma mater?"

Dark suspicions began to form in Rachel's mind, and her gray eyes narrowed. So he hadn't been making love to his editor as she'd been vividly imagining all this time. He'd been much too busy for that. It was obviously no coincidence that he was planning to drag her to Winthrop. Just what did he have in mind?

"You can't expect me to pack up at a moment's notice for one of your whims," she protested.

"Oh, I assure you, this is not a whim," Jason countered. "I've thought it out very carefully."

"Well, I don't give a damn about your careful thinking processes. I'm not going back to Winthrop," she snapped defiantly.

Jason arched a maddening eyebrow. "Afraid?" he questioned.

Rachel felt her face redden. "Certainly not."

"Well, then . . . ?" he prompted

"You know perfectly well why I don't want to go back to Winthrop. It's embarrassing, that's why."

Jason stood up and turned for a moment toward the window as though deep in thought. "Listen, Rachel," he began, and then faced her abruptly once more, "not only is Winthrop an excellent place for me to conduct interviews, but it's also a very good place for you to get in touch with your past and sort out your psyche. After listening to your rationalizations the other evening, I realize how confused you are. And I'd like to give you the chance to clear up some of that confusion. If you don't give yourself this opportunity, you're making a big mistake."

It was Rachel who turned away now and stared blindly at the bookshelves. She didn't know how to respond to what he'd said. Her instincts screamed "Danger." But at the same time, her brain was telling her that maybe he had a point.

She heard him cross the room and stand behind her. But he made no move to touch her. "Besides," he said very quietly, "there will be somebody along on the trip who's on your side."

For a moment she wondered if she'd heard him correctly. But then he added, "You won't be alone. I'll be with you."

His reassuring words tipped the balance. "All right, you win," she agreed in a voice barely above a whisper. "I'll pack my bags."

But later in the day she was struck with the inevitable second thoughts. *How could I let him throw me off balance that way?* she asked herself as she stood before her open closet deciding what to pack. If he had tried to mow her down with the force of his will, she would have resisted. But his unexpected gentleness had undone her. Now she wanted to call him up and back out. Several times she'd even gone to the phone, but she knew if she tried to go against him now, there would be no gentleness in his reaction. His voice would be full of sardonicism at her cowardice. And the realization had made her finger freeze on the dial. Sighing with resignation, she reached out a hand and began to hunt through her wardrobe. If she was going to make this trip, she was going to look her best. It took only a few minutes to select several of her most stylish outfits. When they had been neatly folded in her suitcase, she surveyed them thoughtfully. Then, grinning in sudden amusement, she crossed to the bureau and took out the lacy teddy she'd been saving for a special occasion. Maybe taking it along to Winthrop was a silly whim, but on the other hand anything that would make her feel confident and sophisticated was worth a try.

On the plane to Boston the next morning, she and Jason barely spoke. He seemed preoccupied with the papers he had brought along. Rachel tried to concentrate on the news magazine the pretty blond stewardess had pressed upon her, but it wasn't long before she was staring out the window at the thick layer of clouds that seemed to crowd in upon the jet. The past seemed to crowd in on Rachel too. She dreaded a chance meeting with Dean Mauberry —and with Jonathan, too, for that matter. For months she had assumed she had nothing to say to him. But his love poem had complicated the issue—at least for her. Did he have some notion that they could take up where they had left off? Her stomach began to churn, and she looked blindly down at the magazine again.

As the plane began to make its descent into Logan Airport, Jason turned to her.

"I think I'd better fill you in on the schedule. We'll be going directly to the campus, where I have a series of interviews set up for today. And then tomorrow we're going to visit some classes." Taking in her look of apprehension, Jason added, "Don't worry, Dean Mauberry isn't on your schedule, and you're not likely to run into anybody you don't want to see—today at least."

Rachel's eyebrows drew together in a frown. What did that bode for tomorrow? she wondered. But there was no use worrying about it.

As they waited for her luggage to appear Rachel reflected that at least she and Jason looked the part of a coolly professional research team. In his camel-hair topcoat worn over an expensively cut tweed jacket, Jason was formidably handsome. And in her crisp navy wool blazer and coordinating plaid skirt under her own tan topcoat, Rachel knew she was holding her own.

As they taxied through the tunnel separating the airport from the city, Jason turned to her again and explained crisply, "Since you know your way around the campus, you won't have to waste any time getting oriented. Your first appointments are in Kahler Hall. I'll have the driver drop you off there and take your luggage to the hotel. We can meet back there before dinner."

Rachel agreed to his plan, and the next few hours in the science building sped by in a whirl of activity. Jason had made sure that every minute of the rest of their workday was filled, and when her last interview was finally over, Rachel was exhausted.

The hotel Jason had selected downtown was a pleasant surprise. Instead of the modern plastic motel she'd been expecting to check into, she found herself in a charming restored nineteenth-century lodge. A relic of the great railroad era, the sprawling edifice had languished in Boston's market district until a group of farsighted businessmen had come up with a plan to restore it to its former glories. Now, with its cove ceilings, rich damask draperies, and marble fireplaces in every room, it was a showplace for well-heeled travelers.

Rachel just had time to get back to her charmingly furnished room, take a shower, and change into the soft dove-gray wool dinner dress she'd brought along before Jason tapped on her door. She'd chosen the dress with care, thinking that it struck just the right feminine note without being seductive. It was meant to suggest a kind of remote coolness that she hoped would keep Jason at arm's length.

But the mocking smile that curved his lips when he took in her appearance told her that he'd read her intentions all too accurately and found them highly entertaining.

However, he was the soul of decorum as he escorted her out of the hotel.

"We have reservations at Locke-Ober's," he informed her while the doorman hailed a cab.

She nodded with pleasure, remembering meals at the plush restaurant as being highlights of her stay in Boston.

Jason was at pains to keep the conversation light over their dinners of lobster thermidor and beef tenderloin.

"This is wonderful," she told him, tackling her lobster with enthusiasm. "I've always enjoyed eating in restaurants. But then my mother was never much of a cook."

"I don't really remember what kind of cook my mother was," Jason commented. "She died when I was just a kid."

"Oh, I didn't know," Rachel responded sympathetically. "That must have been tough."

"Yeah," Jason agreed, his thoughts seeming to turn inward for a moment. "I missed her a lot, and the old man wasn't home much after that either."

Rachel threw him a curious glance, wondering what was behind that guarded statement. But she couldn't ask.

Jason looked from his plate and caught the expression of perplexity in her gray eyes. "Some time when I've had a few too many, I may tell you about it. But let's not spoil this particular meal. Your family is probably a safer topic of conversation. What are your folks like?"

Obediently following his lead, she began to describe her doctor father and women's-club mother. But as she spoke, her mind still lingered on Jason's words. For a moment she had glimpsed another man—a vulnerable man below that diamond-hard surface, and she was intrigued. But Jason seemed determined to steer her away from himself. And as the meal drew to a close he became businesslike once again, asking about her day's activities.

Between sips of coffee she gave him a summary of her interviews, while he nodded with interest. "What do you have planned for tomorrow?" she finally asked.

"Oh, that's a surprise," he hedged, his face carefully blank and his blue eyes giving nothing away.

Suddenly apprehensive, Rachel shot him a searching glance.

"Don't worry," he assured her, "it's actually a lighter schedule than today."

She wanted to ask more about his plans for the morning. But the set of his jaw made it clear that the subject was closed. A few minutes later he was calling for the check.

Back in her hotel room Rachel treated herself to a hot relaxing bath in the huge antique claw-footed tub and then flopped limply into bed. She looked around at her posh surroundings but failed to take any cheer now from their luxury. The fireplace, with its gaping black mouth, was depressingly cold and empty. And she stared into its blackness for a long time before she could get to sleep. What did Jason have planned for tomorrow? Did it have anything to do with Jonathan? Or was this feeling of nervous apprehension gnawing at her groundless?

Groundless or not, she woke up with that same uneasy sensation in the morning. Would she be coming face to face with Jonathan? she wondered. She wouldn't put it past Jason to have something like that planned. And if he did, she definitely wanted to look and feel her best.

Rummaging in her suitcase, she pulled out the extravagant lacy teddy she'd bought with Marta.

Why not? she told herself, unbelting her robe and slipping into the luxurious wisp of silky material. Standing before the full-length mirror on the back of the bathroom door, Rachel stared at her image for a moment. The slim, enticing woman in the mirror appeared so unlike her usual self that Rachel almost felt she was looking at a stranger. The peach silk set off her ivory skin, and she could see the sensual curve of her breasts glimmering below the lace openwork where a row of tiny buttons covered her bodice.

Rachel couldn't help grinning. Maybe you didn't know how true it was when you told Marta that these things were sexy, she mused. Even to Rachel's own eyes, the scantily clad woman in the mirror, with her cloud of dark red hair, radiated allure. Striking a pinup-girl pose, she contemplated herself with a mixture of pleasure and amusement. But then her smile faded, and her eyes became thoughtful. *Why am I doing this?* she wondered. No one's going to see it, after all. Quickly she pulled out the tailored outfit she'd selected for the day.

Her white blouse, navy blazer, neat tweed skirt and high-heeled boots quickly camouflaged the sensual image. No one would ever guess what's under this outfit, she thought as she pinned her hair back in its usual neat chignon before applying a light touch of makeup.

During breakfast in the coffee shop, Jason glanced at his watch. "Finish up your English muffin," he admonished, "or we're going to be late for our lecture."

"Lecture?" Rachel questioned, setting down her coffee cup.

"Yes." Jason smiled faintly. "I think it would be a good experience to take in English Three-oh-one."

Rachel froze. "You mean, the survey of Victorian literature?" she asked, her suspicions beginning to take form.

"Exactly." Jason got up, pushing his chair back with a scrape, and took her elbow. "We're going to have to hurry."

As they stepped out under the hotel marquee their faces were lashed by a cutting north wind. The overcast sky seemed to promise snow, and Rachel was glad to scurry into the warmth of the taxi that the doorman promptly hailed.

Settling back into the vinyl upholstery, Rachel tried to smooth her hair. But as she raked her fingers through its russet length, Jason's strong brown hand closed over hers to stop the motion. "I like you windblown," he whispered in her ear. Rachel colored and looked away. Next to her Jason chuckled. "I like you with a little pink in your cheeks too," he added good-humoredly.

What was he up to? Rachel wondered uneasily. These were really the first personal compliments she had received from him in quite a while. But, far from being reassuring, his air of affable accommodation put her on her guard. In fact, she felt her misgivings build during the short cab ride. Sliding Jason a glance, she tried to read something in his face. But his tranquil profile gave nothing away.

They reached Harper Auditorium in Slayton Hall about ten minutes before the lecture was scheduled to begin. The large auditorium was more than three-quarters filled with sophomores and juniors and rang with the sound of their muffled conversations.

"What is it you're trying to do?" Rachel hissed, her agitation growing as Jason guided her firmly to a back seat in a dark corner.

"Just be quiet and watch the show," he directed. Rachel stared straight ahead, her jaw clenched. He had to be the most manipulative, overbearing man she had ever met in her life.

"Now that the lecture hall is nearly filled, it's interesting to notice the composition of the students, don't you think?" Jason asked with deceptive mildness.

"I don't know what you mean," Rachel said stiffly, still refusing to look at him.

"I mean," Jason went on with a great show of patience, "that though Winthrop has a much higher population of males than females, three quarters of the students in here are girls—and all of them are dressed to the teeth. I'd say there must be something rather special about this lecturer. I wonder what it could be."

Rachel's head snapped around. Jason was grinning a toothy crocodile smile that made her want to step on his foot. She knew what he was getting at, all right. "This is an English lecture. There are always more girls majoring in English, so there's nothing unusual about the numbers," she pointed out reasonably, struggling to keep her voice even.

"We'll see," Jason murmured complacently.

Just then a door in the side of the auditorium opened and Jonathan Convers entered. Immediately the chatter which had filled the room lowered to a hushed murmur, and scores of female eyes were trained on the handsome professor as he walked in his sprightly way up to the stage at the front. Like the students, Rachel's eyes were also riveted on him. Seeing him again was like a blow to the stomach. He had been at the center of her thoughts for so long. Before leaving Winthrop, she had worshiped him, and afterward she had brooded about him. And even through her anger and disillusionment, memory had somehow endowed him with an almost superhuman status. Would seeing him in the flesh like this diminish that fantasy picture? she asked herself. She didn't know yet. Her reactions were in too much of a tangle.

It was not quite time for the lecture to start and three or four designer–jean-clad coeds had got up to cluster around the lectern. Even from the back of the room Rachel could hear little bursts of intimate laughter as they bantered with the professor.

"Which one of them do you think is his favorite this year?" Jason leaned over to whisper. "I vote for the blonde with the straight hair and big breasts."

Rachel clenched her teeth and shot him a withering look. But part of her was absorbing the little scene with a transformed perspective. From an outsider's view it did suggest that something more than academics was at work here. Yet, she wasn't going to give Jason an inch. "Jonathan is a very impressive and attractive man. It's not surprising that his female students think so too."

"They're hanging around him like sweat bees in August. And he's certainly not trying to discourage them," Jason drawled maddeningly.

Rachel smiled with false sweetness. "It's really amusing to hear you say that. I certainly haven't noticed you trying to discourage the students who cluster around you."

Jason smiled tightly. "Don't make comparisons till you've seen the rest of the performance. It hasn't really gotten underway yet."

The start of the lecture was delayed slightly as Jonathan kept up what must have been a series of very witty exchanges, judging from the gales of laughter that issued from the front of the auditorium. As the group of girls who had surrounded him finally turned to take their seats, one in particular caught Rachel's eyes. Her long chestnut hair framed a wistfully pretty face dominated by oversize green eyes. Unlike the other chattering coeds in the group, she radiated a sensitivity and vulnerability that set her apart. But it was her expression of almost feverish excitement, when Jonathan casually touched her shoulder as she turned to leave, that galvanized Rachel's attention. *Did I look like that two years ago?* she wondered, wincing involuntarily. The girl obviously had a colossal crush on Jonathan and was too innocent and inexperienced to know how to hide it. *Was she heading for disaster—the same kind of disaster I walked into?* Rachel wondered.

The girl had taken a seat close to the front of the large room, but at an angle where Rachel could see her profile. Jonathan had begun to speak, and the girl's eyes were fixed on him with the rapt intensity of a supplicant adoring the image of a saint.

"I see you've noticed the enraptured novitiate over there," Jason whispered in Rachel's ear. "Convers seems to have a thing for the spiritual type, I see."

Rachel inhaled sharply. "It's not his fault if she admires him," she retorted.

"So you'd argue that he hasn't encouraged it," Jason persisted. "Just look at him, Rachel. So far he's been delivering most of this lecture straight to her."

And it was true, Rachel realized, watching the exchange of warm, lingering glances between master and neophyte. If the girl was hanging on Jonathan's every word, he was looking at her as though she were the only person in the room. His concentration on her was unmistakable, and the other girls were aware of it too. Though she was too transfixed to notice, many were shooting her looks of annoyance and envy.

"Tell me, Rachel, what effect does it have on a student to have a man like Convers single her out that way?" Jason's voice grated in her ear. Though she didn't bother to reply, she knew the answer. A few years ago Jonathan had looked at her that way, she remembered with searing clarity. And though she had certainly been less naive than this girl appeared, her response had been almost as unguardedly worshipful. But now her perspective was quite different. If what she were seeing weren't so pathetic, it would be laughable.

The end of the lecture was much like the beginning. Jonathan exited Slayton Hall surrounded by an adoring group of young women. And the girl with the chestnut hair had a special place of honor at his side. Although Jonathan and his entourage walked right up the aisle where Rachel and Jason were sitting, the professor was far too busy to notice his former student. When they had passed, Jason pulled her out of her seat.

"Let's trail along behind our golden boy," he suggested sarcastically, guiding Rachel firmly with one hand in the small of her back.

They were only a few paces behind Professor Convers and his coterie, and suddenly Rachel became aware of how much taller Jason was than the fair-haired professor, how much broader his shoulders, how much more he projected—even in the darkened lecture hall—an aura of masculine dynamism. Some of the coeds around them had begun to notice it too, Rachel observed. Many were giving him surreptitious glances. And a few were staring at him with open speculation. "Who is that hunk?" Rachel heard one tall brunette whisper to her companion. "I'd sure like

135

to get *him* in a discussion of sexual symbolism in the Victorian poets," the girl with her snickered.

Rachel shot Jason a quick look. But he showed no sign of having heard.

Once in the harsh winter air the group of students began to break up. Some of the girls seemed to hover uncertainly around Rachel and Jason before scattering in several directions. Others stood watching as Jonathan and his chestnut-haired companion began to walk briskly toward the English department offices.

"Well?" Jason asked, staring down at Rachel's frozen features. "Learn anything?"

"If I did, I'm certainly not going to discuss it with you," she retorted, unwilling to let him see how much the morning had enlightened and disturbed her. "Just what did you expect to gain from this didactic little research trip?"

Jason's brows drew together in an angry scowl, and his face darkened. "I expected you to have the maturity to be able to see Jonathan Convers for what he really is—a coed-chasing Lothario like Charles Riddle. You don't think those girls would be sitting there drooling that way unless he'd done an awful lot to encourage them, do you? Come on; admit it."

Rachel's face was stormy. She wasn't prepared to admit a thing—not to Jason Brand anyway. "You are the most arrogant and dictatorial bully I ever met, and I'm not going to stand here letting you manipulate me for another second!"

Without giving him a chance to answer, she turned on her heels and fled up the tree-lined walk, not even aware that she was heading toward the English department. But once she had come face-to-face with the heavy green bronze doors, she automatically pushed them open—anything to escape Jason's mocking stare. Even at this distance she could still feel his derisive gaze burning into her back. Inside the building's shelter, Rachel stood uncertainly in the empty hall gazing around with clouded eyes. How often as a student she had stood in this same spot admiring the ornate plaster ceilings and stately carved walnut doors of the antique building, she thought.

Jonathan's office was on the second floor, and Rachel's feet seemed to take that route up the wide marble steps as though programmed. It made no sense to approach Jonathan now, she reasoned, for her visit to the lecture hall really had changed her perception of him. Although she had not been willing to concede as much to Jason, she was ready to admit that the primary emotion she now felt for him was pity. The adoring crowd of coeds he had deliberately collected around himself had saddened her. How weak his self-esteem must really be, she reasoned, to require that kind of constant gratification. Yet, something still impelled her. Was it a need to punish herself? she wondered. Or was it a determination to finally lay old ghosts to rest?

When she reached Jonathan's half-closed door, however, she stood uncertainly in front of it for a moment. She was about to turn and walk away when the sound of voices drifting through the doorway stopped her.

"I'm very impressed with your paper, Miss Phillips," Jonathan was saying. "This shows a real sensitivity to the mores of the Victorians."

Rachel paused, arrested. Hadn't Jonathan said something almost exactly like that to her once?

"Oh, thank you, Professor Convers," a breathless voice rejoined. "I was so afraid you would think my conclusions lacked depth."

The professor chuckled. "On the contrary I think you have one of the brightest minds in the class, and I'd like to discuss your ideas more extensively. Actually there's a position opening up next year as my research assistant, and I think you might just be the person I'm looking for."

While the coed gasped with pleasure, Rachel stood frozen to the spot. It was like reliving a scene from her own past. Only now she was no longer a participant but a detached observer. She clenched her fists. Part of her wanted to charge into the room, to warn the vulnerable girl of Jonathan's plans for her. But what good would that do? Miss Phillips would never believe her. She was going to have to find out for herself what Jonathan wanted—the hard way. And Rachel could only hope that the girl would emerge from the experience less damaged than she had been.

CHAPTER NINE

Rachel shivered and pulled the collar of her camel-hair coat closer around her throat. She was no longer used to the biting cold of a Boston winter, and a stiff wind had sprung up, sending shivers through her slender body.

Head bent and shoulders hunched, she had been walking for some time—walking blindly without paying any heed to her surroundings. But the penetrating chill of the air was beginning to get through to her.

Where am I? she wondered, raising her head and looking around. The buildings of Winthrop University were now to her right, and the Charles River shimmered behind her like a silver strand of Christmas tinsel. Unconsciously she had been heading back toward her hotel.

Was Jason waiting for her there? she wondered, glancing at her watch. Although she had not been conscious of time passing, it was already after lunch, and he might well be out on interviews again. And if he hadn't bothered to wait for her, who could blame her? Her eyes were bleak as she remembered how she had given him a tongue-lashing this morning and turned her angry back to follow Jonathan. But Rachel acknowledged now that, even as she had clung fiercely to those tattered shreds of denial, she must have suspected what she would encounter at Jonathan's office door.

As Rachel pressed on, large wet flakes of snow began to swirl out of the gray sky. *Whether Jason's there or not, I'd better get back to the hotel,* she told herself, shivering dejectedly.

How ironic, she reflected, as she let a strong current of frigid air push her forward. She knew now what man she wanted to be with—and it wasn't Jonathan Convers. It was Jason Brand. With sudden insight she admitted to herself that she had unconsciously been comparing the two men for months. But her romanticized memory of Jonathan had been so much safer than the dynamic, masculine reality of Jason that she had always fled into the past. Old habits die hard, even when they are ultimately self-destructive, she realized now. But today all that had been swept away.

She was finally free to admit her feelings for Jason Brand. When he had made it clear that he wanted her, she had been afraid. But now her fears seemed childish. Would her hard-won insights today help her meet him on a more mature level? She hoped it wasn't too late.

Turning the corner, Rachel hurried through the now rapidly falling snowflakes past the taxis waiting at the circular drive in front of the hotel. Another gust of wind propelled her through the wide glass and burnished metal doors into the lobby. Stopping at the desk, she asked if there had been any messages and turned away in disappointment when the clerk answered in the negative. Jason

140

was probably out interviewing, after all, and hadn't bothered to leave word of his whereabouts. Why should he? After her behavior this morning, he was probably thoroughly disgusted with her. With leaden steps she headed for the elevator, hoping that the maid had had a chance to make up the bed and tidy her room. If she waited there long enough, Jason was bound to check in with her sometime.

Wearily Rachel turned her key in the lock, pushed open the door, and stepped into the room. For a moment she felt disoriented. In the marble fireplace a neat stack of logs blazed a warm greeting. Nearby a round table set with snowy linen and gleaming silver cutlery waited beside a serving cart of covered dishes set over small burners. And in the wingback chair by the window sat Jason Brand, one cordovan-clad foot resting comfortably on the opposite knee of his tweed slacks. Pencil in hand, he was making notations on a stack of interview forms in his lap.

As she advanced into the room he set the forms down on the end table and gave her a slow smile. "I thought you might be hungry. So I waited lunch," he observed calmly.

Completely taken by surprise, Rachel could only gape at him for a moment. "But it's—it's way past lunchtime," she finally stammered.

"Better late than never," he pointed out, rising from his seat and quickly crossing the room toward her. "Here, let me help you off with your coat, and then you can warm up in front of the fire."

Rachel let him slip the garment off her shoulder before moving toward the hearth. This reception was the last thing she had expected.

"I didn't know the fireplaces here really worked," she

commented, suddenly unaccountably shy. "What a stroke of luck."

"Oh, they work, all right," Jason rejoined. "It's getting the staff to cooperate and bring up the wood that's a minor miracle." As he spoke he uncorked a bottle of rosé, poured two long-stemmed glasses, and handed one to Rachel. "Another step in the thawing-out process," he explained.

Rachel took a small sip and then another. "It's wonderful," she acknowledged.

"Let's hope the food is as good," Jason agreed after sampling his wine.

Rachel turned back to the fire again, pretending to be absorbed with the dancing flames. Her mind was in a spin—like the swirling snow outside that had now practically obliterated the view from the window.

Her last encounter with Jason had been harsh and angry. Now he was all solicitousness and charm. Was it some sort of ploy? Or did he know instinctively what she needed after the searing experience of the morning? Whatever the reason, she accepted his consideration gratefully.

Instinctively she knew he was offering her more than lunch this afternoon. He had made the offer before. And she had always refused. But now everything was suddenly different. She was no longer under the spell of the past. Watching Jonathan's performance at the lecture and hearing him turn on the charm in his office had done their work. She had been punishing herself all along for something that had not been her fault. Jonathan had led her on. She could see that now. And she knew that if he had really cared for her, he would have tried to help heal her emotional wounds.

Without Jason's careful preparation the realization would have been shattering. Even in the face of her strong resistance, he had made it possible for her to be free again. And it suddenly felt so very good, as if she had just awakened from a long drugged slumber.

Well, if I've been Sleeping Beauty, Rachel told herself, *Jason has been playing the part of the Prince.* His kisses had begun the process of arousing her. And this trip to Boston of his had completed the process. Feeling a surge of emotion, Rachel turned around to face Jason. She didn't know what the future held for the two of them. But she could no longer repress the feelings he aroused in her. And she suddenly wanted very much to experience the present to the fullest with him. After two stagnant years of brooding over a man unworthy of her tender emotions, she owed it to herself. And in a way she owed it to Jason too. For he was the man who had set her free.

"Ready to eat?" Jason asked, and Rachel nodded. Slipping out of her navy blazer, she hung it on the back of her chair and then pulled off her wet boots before sitting down.

Jason took his own seat across from her. Uncovering several serving dishes, he revealed a platter of sirloin steak tips in red wine sauce, wild rice with fresh mushroom slices, and string beans almandine. Tempting aromas drifted toward Rachel.

"I'll do the honors," Jason said, as he filled a plate and handed it to her. Then he served himself.

Rachel watched him in wonder. He seemed able to ignore completely the events of the morning, as if the two of them had just arrived at this pleasant hotel for a quiet vacation—a lovers' tryst, she added to herself, taking a deep breath. Perhaps at the moment that was just what she needed.

Rachel carefully cut off a small piece and began to eat.

The meat was as delicious as its aroma, delicately spiced with thyme and rosemary and the robust kiss of the red wine. Leaning back in her chair, she cut another piece and then sampled the tangy wild rice.

While she ate, she glanced often at Jason, watching him butter a slice of French bread from the basket on the table and then turn to his own main course. She took in anew, as if seeing them for the first time, his large powerful hands, his well-shaped mouth, the strong line of his jaw as he chewed, and the way his dark hair swept across his forehead. He was eating with obvious relish. But that was how he did everything. He was a man who knew how to enjoy life. Was it too late to learn that art from him?

"It's all so good," she offered. "Thank you for arranging all this, Jason."

He acknowledged her appreciation with an engaging smile and then pushed back his chair. "Let me stir up the fire."

As he expertly wielded the poker Rachel followed the ripple of strong muscles under his crisp Oxford-cloth shirt. An odd feeling was beginning to overtake her, as if her world were contracting to include only this room, this man.

Unconsciously she leaned forward toward Jason. And when he straightened up and turned away from the fireplace, he came to stand beside her chair.

"Let's have our coffee on the sofa," he suggested softly, taking her elbow and helping her to her feet. It was the first time he had touched her since she entered the room, and the brief contact with his strong fingers, through the silky material of her blouse, was electric. Had Jason felt it too? she wondered. But he made no comment as he took

144

up the silver coffeepot and poured two cups of the dark, aromatic drink.

"Cream and sugar?" he asked, his eyes full upon her face.

Rachel hesitated only an instant. "Yes," she said finally. In that moment she knew he had really been asking her a different question. And her answer had carried with it a much richer, more important meaning. She shivered slightly in anticipation as she accepted the cup from his outstretched hand. The atmosphere in the room was heavy with luxuriant promise.

They sat for a moment in silence, each sipping the hot liquid. Then Jason casually set his cup on the table and just as casually took Rachel's from her hand. His blue eyes had turned the deep cobalt of twin volcanic-crater lakes as he carefully set her cup beside his own. For a long moment he didn't move. And then, with one extended finger, he reached up to trace delicately the line of her jaw and then the outline of her lips. Prickles of electric heat followed his touch, and Rachel's mouth opened slightly. Jason's finger slipped inside and began ever so slowly to caress the sensitive inner surface of her lips.

Giving herself up to the exquisite sensation, Rachel closed her eyes and leaned back into the soft cushions of the couch. When his finger paused, she ran her tongue along its length, lingering at the tip to explore his smooth fingernail.

After a moment, he withdrew the finger with slow deliberation and reached up to caress her cheek with the palm of his hand. "I want you to open your eyes and look at me," he whispered, his warm breath feathering her ear.

Obediently Rachel raised her lids and found her gray eyes locked with his fathomless blue ones.

"You're not going to stop me this time, are you?" he asked.

"No," she murmured, acknowledging her surrender not only to this man but to some powerful inevitable force that had been building inside her for a long time.

His lips descended then to capture hers. And again she opened the moist sweetness of her mouth to his exploration. Why had she resisted so long? Rachel wondered. She could think of no good reason now. It felt so right to be here in Jason's arms at last.

His hands were at the back of her hair, loosening the pins that held her chignon in place. One by one he withdrew them, and then began to comb his fingers through her red hair until it hung in a thick fiery cascade around her shoulders.

"Rachel, you're so sexy this way," he murmured, nuzzling his face against her hair and neck. And it was true. She felt as though a floodgate of pent-up sensuality had finally been released.

Jason began dropping light, quick kisses against her cheek, her forehead, her eyelids. It was like a rain of liquid fire on her already fevered skin. And she wanted more. Eagerly she reached up to caress the back of his neck and twine her own fingers in his dark hair.

"For months I've wanted you to do that—and so much more." He groaned, clasping her hand and tenderly kissing the quickening pulse at her wrist.

There was no thought of protest this time when his searching fingers found the buttons of her blouse. In a moment he had pushed the silky fabric back from her shoulders and bent his lips to kiss the warm V of her cleavage. Then his supple hands were on her breasts, lifting and caressing them through the sheer fabric of her

146

teddy before seeking out her hardened nipples. His fingers teased and excited them through the whisper-thin barrier, sending an electric thrill deep within her, and Rachel's back arched. A low moan escaped from her lips as her whole body throbbed with anticipation.

She felt his arms then, under her hips and shoulders. Lifting her pliant desire-roused body with ease, he carried her across the room and laid her gently on the bed before reaching for the clasp of her skirt and pulling the unwanted garment down over her legs.

Through half-closed eyes she watched him regarding her reclining form, now clad only in the lacy teddy, with a mixture of delight and puzzlement.

"That thing you're wearing is damn sexy-looking," he drawled. "But how the hell do you get it off?"

Rachel couldn't repress a wicked grin. "So you're not as experienced as I thought you were," she teased, her gray eyes now wide with innocence.

Her own hands went to the row of tiny buttons at the front of the teddy. And, eyes locked on Jason's face, she began one by one to unfasten them. Enjoying the sensation of her own seductive power, she studied the look of smoldering passion in his blue eyes, knowing that she was exciting him beyond endurance.

"You want to drive me crazy, don't you?" he groaned, his voice rough with desire. And then he was beside her on the bed, his hands urgently pushing the straps of the wispy garment off her shoulders and sliding it down her body. "My God, you're beautiful," he muttered huskily. "Your skin is like ivory in the firelight. Oh, Rachel, I want you so much."

His own clothing quickly joined her teddy in a tangled heap at the foot of the bed. And then, with studied sensuality, he bent to caress her with his hands and lips—tracing the line of her hip, feathering kisses across her abdomen, circling her nipples with delicious little strokes that made them hard as pearls. Rachel moaned, glorying in the strong surge of passion that raged through her fevered body.

She knew now what it was like to be fully alive, nerve endings afire with the overwhelming sensations Jason was producing.

With mounting passion she combed her fingers through the thick mat of hair on his chest and pressed her lips to the strong cords of his neck.

And when she felt his searching fingers on the sensitive skin of her inner thigh, she opened herself to him, to her most intimate recesses.

"Ah, you're so warm and ready for me," he murmured.

And it was true. He had turned the core of her being to an aching liquid flame.

Urgently she began to move her hips in concert with his probing, stroking fingers. "Oh, darling," she whispered, her voice thick with desire, "I want you."

Jason propped himself on one elbow, his cobalt blue eyes burning down into hers. "Another man might make you wait," he muttered hoarsely. "The way you made me wait for this afternoon. But it's beyond my self-control."

Her breath was coming in short broken little gasps now as her hands roamed urgently over his body. It was with a sigh of relief that she felt his muscular frame shift onto hers. She saw passion flare in his eyes, and then their bodies were joined in the complete embrace they both sought so passionately.

Rachel cried out in pleasure and then marveled as the pleasure increased, taking her higher and higher in a spiral of overwhelming sensations she had never dreamed of. She was like a butterfly caught in an updraft, soaring above the treetops, above the mountains, above even the clouds. The flight carried her to unbelievable peaks. And she cried out again in the all-consuming ecstasy of her release.

Jason pulled her into the circle of his arms and nuzzled his face tenderly against her hair and neck. "You were worth waiting for," he whispered.

In answer Rachel snuggled closer against the muscled wall of his chest.

The fire had died down, and Jason pulled the bedcovers up around their shoulders. With the snow swirling outside, they might have been two bears in a cave turning to each other for warmth during the long winter night. Sighing, Rachel closed her eyes and let herself drift in the comforting warmth of Jason's embrace. Yes, she agreed silently, this had been worth waiting for.

It was hours later that she awoke. Darkness had fallen, and she could just make out the dark outline of Jason propped up on his elbow looking down at her.

"Hungry?" he asked. And Rachel realized that she was.

"Starving," she agreed, stretching luxuriously and then hastily pulling the sheet up as she realized her nakedness.

But Jason wouldn't allow her to hide. He reached down deliberately and grazed the tips of her exposed breasts with his lips and then smiled into her eyes. As her nipples hardened under his touch, he chuckled with male satisfaction. "Eat first and then make love later?" he offered, pushing the covers back and striding toward the bathroom. Rachel's eyes followed the lithe, muscular line of his naked body, which had, it occurred to her, the grace of a Greek athlete's. He was beautiful, she thought.

In a moment she heard the shower running, and then

his deep voice singing out over the pounding spray, "Come on in. The water's fine."

With a blush Rachel remembered how she had imagined just such a scene after reading his journal. She wasn't quite ready for that yet and waited sedately in bed until he emerged from the bathroom to turn it over to her.

Thirty minutes later Rachel was garbed once more in her dove-gray dinner dress, her fiery hair loose around her shoulders instead of pulled back in its conservative chignon. And there was nothing conservative about her emotions as she swayed down the hall toward the elevator with Jason's arm wrapped firmly around her. Anyone looking at them would know they were lovers, she mused. But she could not draw away from him.

Jason asked for a corner table with a wide banquette where the two of them could sit side by side in relative privacy. The snowstorm had kept diners from the outside at home, and the baroquely elegant restaurant was frequented now only by guests of the hotel.

This time the pressure of Jason's hard thigh against her own was a delicious reminder of the intimacy they had just shared and a promise of what would happen between them later on. And Rachel, caught in the net of golden sensuality Jason had woven around her, was more than complacent at the thought. His mesmeric effect on her was so complete that she hardly noticed what he ordered for them and ate the delicately sautéed scampi and crisp spinach salad that materialized before her in a haze. The focus of Jason's attention seemed far away from the meal also. Not long after the food had been served, she felt his hand exploring the softness of her thigh under the smooth wool of her dress. And when she looked up into his eyes, they were burning into her like blue fire.

Leaning her head against his shoulder, she instinctively moved closer, allowing his hand to move even higher.

"Let's get out of here," Jason whispered gruffly into her ear, pushing away his half-finished plate. "It's not food I want right now."

"Yes," Rachel agreed, her voice laced with desire.

Jason tossed a pile of bills on the tablecloth, and together they quickly made their way back to the elevators.

Once inside the room, Jason hauled Rachel against his hard body so that she could feel his arousal. "I want you so much," he groaned, his hands going to the zipper at the back of her dress and sliding it easily down. As the wool slipped from her shoulders, revealing the creamy skin beneath, Jason's burning lips descended to Rachel's shoulders, her neck, her throat, the tops of her breasts just visible above her lacy bra. And as his mouth moved over her in insistent demand, wavelets of fire seemed to race over her skin. She felt herself melting against him like a rapidly burning candle. Urgently her fingers sped to the buttons of his shirt and began to slide them open as her mouth sought the hard surface of the muscles of his chest. Jason's reaction was furnacelike as her questing lips and teeth stoked his passion. Convulsively his leg pushed against hers; his hands cupped her buttocks, pulling them hard against the structure of his hips. She moaned against his mouth, aroused beyond any conscious thought now. And in the next instant Jason swept her into his arms and carried her back to the passion-tousled bed that was waiting for them.

CHAPTER TEN

Pale sunlight on Rachel's closed eyelids woke her up. For a moment she was disoriented, and then hot color flooded her cheeks as she recalled vividly the events of the afternoon and night before. Jason had made passionate and demanding love to her over and over through the night and as she pushed herself up in bed, she found that her body ached slightly from his attentions.

Instinctively her head turned to the side of the bed that his lean male form had occupied, but it was cold and empty. Only the rumpled sheet and depression in the pillow case testified that he had been there. She listened for the sound of the shower, but the room was empty. He must have returned to his own room, she thought, to change his clothes. With an oddly hollow sensation in her chest, Rachel swung her long legs over the side of the bed and reached for a robe to cover her nakedness. Her dress and underwear lay scattered in careless heaps across the flowered rug, and the sight was somehow distressing.

Leaning over, she began to gather them up. Smoothing out the dove-gray fabric and shaking out her crumpled slip, she began to tidy the evidence of last night's heedless ardor.

As her eyes swept the room, she noticed a piece of paper on the table next to the bed. It was a note from Jason:

> Have an early appointment this morning that I can't miss. Sleep late, and I'll meet you after lunch.
>
> Jason

No *Love, Jason,* she noted—just his name and the bald explanation of his absence. Well, what had she expected. He'd never pretended to be in love with her. Even during their night of passion, he'd never mentioned the word *love.* It had always been clear that what he wanted was an affair. And if she were honest, that was all that had been in her mind yesterday too. But now she knew it wasn't enough. She had really been in love with Jason for a long time now. And last night she had admitted it to herself—finally and completely. Now the fact that he was so obviously not in love with her made cold shivers of misery circulate through her blood.

Crumpling the note, she let it slip through her fingers into the wastebasket beside the table. And then, her clouded eyes averted from the bed, she went into the bathroom and began running the water for her shower.

Jason had indicated he wouldn't be back for lunch. And so, after dressing in her blazer and plaid skirt, Rachel went down to the hotel's coffee shop for a late brunch. However, the cheese omelet and toast she unenthusiastically ordered seemed to stick in her throat, and she found herself pushing the half-eaten meal away. Turning her coffee cup around in the saucer, she watched the swirl of dark liquid. What's wrong with you, Rachel? she asked herself. You've made a mess of things again. Why can't you fall in love with someone who can reciprocate? And what's the future going to be like with Jason? Do you really want to carry on a pointless affair, just waiting for the moment when he'll tire of you? The answer to that, she knew, was no. Last night she had been willing to grasp at the happiness of being Jason's lover. But now that she recognized her true feelings for him, she knew she couldn't settle for the merely casual affair that he so obviously wanted.

But there was more than that problem to cope with. What was she going to do about her job? Knowing that she was going to refuse to continue the affair, how could she go on working with Jason? It was impossible. The whole situation was impossible. With a sinking sensation Rachel acknowledged to herself that, when they got back to Quincy Adams, she was going to have to bail out. The realization seemed to drain her of what little vitality she still possessed. Suddenly she felt a leaden exhaustion settle over her like a crushing weight. Glancing up at the clock on the wall she saw it was only eleven thirty A.M. But it might as well have been midnight.

Dragging herself back up to her room, she removed her blazer and shoes and flopped onto the bed, still wearing the rest of her outfit. In seconds she had fallen into a heavy and restless sleep.

It was the touch of strong hands grasping her shoulders and shaking her that brought her back to consciousness.

"For God's sake, Rachel, what are you doing? You're not even packed! Get moving, or we'll miss our plane."

Groggily she looked up into Jason's accusing eyes. Irritation and impatience were written on his face. Brusquely he turned from her and pulled her suitcase out of the closet. Then he began opening drawers and stuffing clothes inside.

"Get your toilet articles out of the bathroom," he commanded curtly. "Don't you know there's been a big snowstorm? I spent the whole damn morning wading through a foot of snow to get to the university only to find that the jerk of a professor I was supposed to meet couldn't get in from Wakefield." Jason scowled heavily as he jammed one of her slips into the tangled heap he'd made of her clothing. "Of course, he didn't bother to call and tell me until I'd been cooling my very wet heels in the sociology department anteroom for over an hour and a half."

Chilled by his tone, Rachel reacted with anger. "Well, you don't have to take it out on my wardrobe," she muttered as she disappeared into the bathroom.

That unpleasant exchange seemed to set the tone between them for the rest of the afternoon. They just barely made it to the airport on time to catch their plane.

"Baltimore?" Rachel exclaimed when she saw the destination printed on their ticket. "Would you mind telling me why we're going to Baltimore?"

"I have to stop by my father's house and pick up a few things," Jason explained tersely, not even bothering to look up from the papers he was frowning over.

Rachel began to seethe. Was this high-handed dictator the same man who had made such tender love to her the night before? It was unbelievable!

The storm had blanketed the whole East Coast, but if conditions had been bad in Boston, they were much worse in Baltimore. Although a lighter snow had fallen, cleaning crews seemed less able to cope with the mess. The ride in the rental car from Baltimore–Washington International

Airport to the rambling stucco house in Baltimore's comfortable Homewood area, where Jason had grown up, was an ordeal. Twice their fenders were nearly crumpled by drivers trying unsuccessfully to maneuver through the uncleared streets. And once Jason himself skidded on a hidden patch of ice. His face was set in a grim mask as he helped her out of the car and showed her up the walk.

"At least you've got boots," he muttered, looking ruefully down at his ruined leather loafers. But Rachel was in no mood to sympathize. His whole attitude this day had been like an unexpected swim in icy water, and the weather seemed only to underline the fact.

It was several minutes before the door was finally opened by a short elderly woman with a thick plait of gray hair coiled on the top of her head.

"Jason!" she exclaimed in surprise, a smile of delight spreading across her wrinkled face. "Why didn't you let us know you were coming?"

"I didn't know myself," he explained, leaning forward to give her a bear hug. "How are you, Vinnie? And how's the old man?"

The woman gave a derisive snort as she stood aside to let Jason and Rachel enter. "Right in character—in fact, he isn't even home. He called up from the apartment of one of his students to tell me he wouldn't be eating dinner here tonight."

Jason's mouth turned down cynically, but he made no comment, and Rachel was left to draw her own conclusions. Had Jason been so perceptive about Jonathan Convers because he was accustomed to the same behavior in his own father? she wondered.

Vinnie was eyeing Rachel speculatively, and as Jason bent to shake snow out of his shoes he began the introductions. "Vinnie, this is Rachel Pritchard, my research assistant. Rachel, this is Lavinia Morgan, the woman who's been the mainstay of this crazy household for the past thirty years and the person who kept my father from murdering me when I was a teenager."

Vinnie laughed in self-deprecation. "Don't give me so much credit, Jason. You were big enough to defend yourself by the time you were fifteen. And the professor has always been too busy with his own affairs to pay all that much attention to your nonsense."

"True enough," Jason conceded dryly, taking Rachel's coat and draping it over the banister to dry.

"You two must be half frozen," Vinnie observed solicitously. "Let me make you a cup of that hot chocolate you're so fond of."

"That sounds wonderful," Jason acknowledged. "Why don't you warm Rachel up in the kitchen for a few minutes? I need to get something upstairs, and then I'll join you."

Rachel allowed herself to be led down a short hall that opened into a large formal dining room furnished with Hepplewhite furniture and Oriental rugs. Struck by the formal beauty of the inlaid woods and shield-back chairs, she paused to look around with admiration. How did one manage to acquire valuable antiques like these on a professor's salary? Rachel wondered.

Her unspoken question was answered by Vinnie. "All these things were inherited from Jason's grandparents. The Brands were an old Baltimore shipping family, you know."

Rachel hadn't known. And as her gaze drifted around the room she was suddenly riveted by the large portrait hanging behind the hunt buffet. Framed in weathered wood and definitely modern in style, the painting was at odds with the formal lines of the furniture. The scene was a nautical one, depicting an older but very well-preserved silver-haired man holding the tiller of a sailboat and gazing off into the sunset. His well-muscled tanned body was naked from the waist up, and the mat of silver hair on his chest was brightened by a gold medallion on a thick chain.

Vinnie chuckled as she followed the direction of Rachel's scrutiny. "Yes, that's the old man."

"Jason's father?" Rachel asked, turning an inquiring look at the housekeeper. But she already felt sure of the answer. The resemblance between Jason and the figure in the portrait was unmistakable, though the differences were also apparent. The man in the painting had struck what was obviously a self-consciously macho pose that Rachel couldn't imagine Jason trying to duplicate. Jason's masculinity was a natural part of him, whereas this man had obviously gone to a great deal of trouble to convey a particular impression of himself.

"What do you think of it?" Vinnie inquired.

Rachel was at a loss for words. She didn't want to offend, after all. But she couldn't bring herself to lie either. "Technically it's quite good, and it has a lot of atmosphere," she finally hedged.

Vinnie snorted. "One of his lady friends painted that," she confided. "Jason told the old man it makes him look like an over-the-hill beach boy. But at least it's better than the one with the long hair and love beads that used to hang there. Of course, the first thing his father did after Jason's comment was make sure he left the portrait to him in his will. But they're always like that with each other," she went on, warming to the subject. "After Jason's mother died, there was no one but me to keep peace in the house.

And neither one of them listens to me unless they want to. It's a wonder the two of them survived those years, the way they went on sometimes. Once when Jason was a teenager he marched into the professor's room when he was entertaining a girl young enough to be Jason's sister. What a blowup there was after that! The old man jumped out of bed naked as a jaybird and grabbed a pistol from his dresser drawer. It wasn't long after that that Jason dropped out of school to join the Special Forces."

Rachel stared at Vinnie in astonishment while she took in this new bit of information. It explained a lot about him, she realized. No wonder Jason was so down on his father. And no wonder he had reacted so violently to her past relationship with Jonathan. And what about his present affair with her? Was it somehow part of the same pattern? Had taking her away from Jonathan been a strange kind of blow at his father? Now that he had succeeded, had he suddenly lost all interest in her? Certainly his behavior today was anything but that of a lover. Suddenly Rachel was sure she had found an important missing piece to the Jason Brand puzzle, and her heart sank.

Vinnie was already pushing open the heavy paneled door to the kitchen, and Rachel followed with a distracted air. "Sit down and I'll fix you a hot drink," the elderly woman offered, gesturing to a wooden trestle table flanked by captain's chairs. Like the rest of the house, the kitchen showed its age. But the tall wooden cabinets, old-fashioned drainboard, and worn quarry tile floor were all spotless.

"It must be quite a job keeping this place up," Rachel observed, trying to make polite conversation.

"Oh, I don't have anything else to do. And since Jason's father spends so little time at home these days, there really

159

isn't a lot of cleaning. If he didn't feel some sense of obligation, he'd probably fire me."

Rachel watched the old woman bustle about, measuring milk, cocoa powder, and sugar into a dented saucepan.

"Things have changed a lot," Vinnie continued, bending to rummage in a lower drawer for a wooden spoon. "I was here before Jason was born, and I took care of him after his mother died when he was eleven." She sighed. "What a job that was! For all the times he and his father were always on the outs, they're really very much alike in a lot of ways. Both of them like the ladies." Vinnie shot Rachel a conspiratorial wink. "But I suspect a pretty young woman like yourself has already discovered that."

Rachel stiffened. What was that supposed to mean? she wondered, but didn't have the nerve to ask.

Just then the door swung open, and the subject of the conversation himself sauntered into the kitchen and pulled out a chair at the table. His mood seemed to have lightened considerably, Rachel noted, taking in his broad smile as he accepted the steaming mug of hot chocolate Vinnie had set at his place. Averting her eyes, Rachel stared blindly down at her own drink. Though the sweet-smelling steam was wafting up to touch her cheeks, she felt cold and out of place.

"Haven't you been taking good care of your research assistant, Jason? She looks pale," Vinnie accused.

Jason shot Rachel an amused glance. "Don't worry, I've been taking very good care of her."

Rachel felt herself redden. It was as though Jason were baldly bragging of his latest conquest to an old confidant, and she felt humiliated. Would this horrible day never end? she asked herself. Right now she wanted nothing more than to be safely back in her own apartment to lick her wounds. What a fool she'd been to let this man add her to the notches on his belt.

Rachel would have liked the ride back to Washington to pass in a numb blur. She wanted to draw into herself, wrapped in her own feelings of misery. But Jason would not allow her that kind of privacy. Vinnie's hot chocolate seemed to have acted on him like a magic potion.

"Sorry I was such a grouch this afternoon," he apologized as he guided the car onto the Baltimore–Washington Parkway. "The snowstorm set me off, I'm afraid, and coming back to my father's house is always a downer for me."

"Then why did you want to stop here?" Rachel mumbled tightly.

Though she refused to look at him, his blue eyes were twinkling mischievously. "There was something important I had to pick up."

"Oh," Rachel answered in a monosyllable, hoping to end the conversation.

However, Jason seemed determined to get back on their old footing and kept up a constant stream of witty conversation. But as the drive proceeded he began to notice how unresponsive Rachel had become.

"Aren't you feeling well, Rachel?" he asked with concern as they drew up in front of her apartment house. "I thought I'd take you out to dinner, but if you're not feeling up to it, I can just come in, bundle you into bed, and fix something light while you rest."

Rachel reacted as though she'd been stung. Her head swung around sharply, and she shot him a look of fury. "I'll just bet you'd like to bundle me into bed," she snapped. "Well, not tonight."

161

Jason's face darkened, and he began to scowl. "What's wrong? You've been acting like a block of ice all day."

"Ice," Rachel exclaimed. "I only wish that were true!"

Jason gave her a level look. "Don't be this way, Rachel. I thought we'd finally stopped playing games with each other yesterday. I wanted to make love to you then, and you damn well seemed to want the same thing. Or was all that passion you showed me simply a balm for your deflated self-esteem? Were you just using me to get over your precious Jonathan?"

Rachel felt her body go rigid with insult and fury. "I don't think that deserves an answer," she replied haughtily. And before he could respond, she threw open the door, stepped out of the car, and began to march up the steps to her apartment. But her grand exit was ruined by Jason's coldly amused voice.

"How about taking your suitcase along?" he prompted caustically.

Rachel shot him a murderous look. "What's the difference? You probably ruined everything you stuffed into it." Nevertheless, she descended again to the sidewalk and stood in frigid silence while he unloaded her case from the trunk.

"Listen, Rachel, this is ridiculous," he began, setting the blue leather bag on the sidewalk. "I don't even know what we're arguing about. Let me come in with you, and we'll settle this right now."

But Rachel had no intention of allowing him into her apartment. She knew that last night's mistake would only be repeated if she did. But even through her anger and hurt, she watched him hungrily as he ran a hand through his tousled hair. She knew that all he had to do was touch her and she would melt in his arms. And she wasn't going to allow that to happen. Seizing the handle of her suitcase, she turned on her heels. "What you want and what I want are two entirely different things, Jason," she flung over her shoulder.

The only answer she received was the roar of a car engine and the squeal of tires as the object of her scorn pulled furiously away from the curb.

CHAPTER ELEVEN

Inside her apartment Rachel looked around with despair. Her emotions were still in turmoil. At least when she had been in the car with Jason, she had been able to channel her violent feelings into anger against him. But now that he was gone, a kind of gray misery began to settle over her mind.

Putting down her suitcase, she walked into the kitchen, filled the teakettle with water, and set it on to boil. She didn't really want anything to drink, but going through the familiar motions was at least something to do. After it was accomplished, however, Rachel stared blankly down at the stove, wondering disjointedly what to do next. *I guess I can unpack,* she told herself, picking up the suitcase again and carrying it toward the bedroom.

As she laid the blue leather bag on the bed and opened it to remove her things, she remembered how she'd felt when she'd first packed it. Then her thoughts had been focused on a possible confrontation with Jonathan. The prospect that she would wind up in Jason's bed hadn't even occurred to her. Or had it? Why had she packed such a sexy wisp of underwear? she asked herself, removing the lacy teddy from the tangled heap of clothing that Jason had jammed into her bag earlier that day. The touch of her fingers on the silky material released a flood of vivid memories—Jason slipping the pencil-thin straps from her shoulders, his lips searing a path of desire across her quivering flesh, his hands awakening her body to heated need. He had made her ache for the fulfillment of his lovemaking, and even now she felt the warmth of her desire for him spread through her veins. It was a feeling she had never come close to with any other man—certainly her fruitless love for Jonathan had come nowhere near the deep emotions rocking her now.

It wasn't just the physical need, she knew. What she had felt for Jonathan had been only a pale imitation of what she now felt for Jason. That naive emotion had only been a preparation for the flowering of her mature feelings. This was real love and if it had a chance to grow and bloom, it would send its strong tendrils into every corner of her life. *But how can I allow that to happen?* Rachel asked herself miserably. He doesn't love me and never did. He's just like Jonathan and probably his father too—all men like that want from women is a series of meaningless affairs.

And in a way, Rachel admitted to herself, the temptation was overpowering. She wanted desperately to make love with him again, to have his arms around her and feel his strength. And perhaps if she gave him what he wanted, he might eventually return some of the deeper, more enduring feelings she had for him. But it was just too much of a chance to take. More than likely the aftermath of their affair would simply be pain and humiliation for her. She had survived something like this once, and she knew she wasn't strong enough to go through it again. She had thought the emotional stakes were high before, but now she had to take herself out of the game. She simply couldn't cover this astronomical a bet.

Rachel was automatically smoothing the wrinkles from her gray wool dress when a shrill burst of sound from the kitchen made her stiffen and jump. Then she remembered the teakettle. She had been so distracted when she'd come in that she'd forgotten about it completely. Laying the dress on the bed, she hurried back to the kitchen, turned the burner off, and set the screaming kettle down on the stove. She didn't really want a cup of tea anyway.

But then what did she want? She couldn't deal with that question yet. To forestall the decision she knew was necessary, she went back to the bedroom to finish unpacking. Then, changing into jeans and a sweat shirt, she busied herself around the apartment with a number of routine chores. Finally, when there was nothing left to vacuum or dust, she sat down on the couch. Though her gray eyes were focused on nothing in particular, a great deal was happening inside her head. *I've got to get away from Jason,* she thought. *I don't know what else to do.* She had momentarily considered sticking out the research, which would be done in about a month's time. But that was impossible. She was going to have to leave and think about the future later. What's more, she knew she couldn't face Jason again. Her mind shied away from the image of a confrontation like a terrified deer fleeing from a mountain cat.

Early tomorrow morning she would go to the office. It would be deserted on the weekend, and she would have time to clear out her desk and leave him a note. Perhaps it was the coward's way out, but right now it seemed like the best method to end this situation with the minimum of unpleasantness. Of course, there was one more problem —Jason's persistence. He'd shown her how he reacted to opposition. He still wanted her, and he was not a man to take no for an answer. He might well come to her apartment; and if he did, would she have the strength to resist him?

She already knew the answer to that. Even now she felt herself weakening as his heart-stopping image began to fill her mind.

"No," she said aloud, reaching for the phone. "If he comes here, he won't find me." In a moment she had dialed Marta's number.

"Rachel, how are you?" the other woman's bubbly voice came over the line. "I didn't know you were back from Boston. How was the trip?"

Rachel grimaced into the receiver, wondering how she was going to put her request. "That's what I want to talk to you about," she began.

But Marta didn't let her finish the sentence. "Is something wrong, Rachel?"

Rachel paused and then went on tentatively, "Marta, there is a problem. I need your help. I know this is a terrible imposition, but I wonder if I could sleep on your couch for the next couple of days?"

There was a shocked silence on the other end of the line. "Rachel. . . ."

Now that Rachel had got the request out, she wondered how in the world she was going to explain. "In Boston—" She floundered. "That is, Jason and I—" She stopped again. "He's going to want to see me after he gets the note, but I just can't see him. . . ."

167

Marta's voice was concerned. "Rachel, you sound terrible and I wish I could let you stay here. But, uh, but— Tom is spending the weekend with me."

Rachel could hear her friend's embarrassment. She gulped. "Oh, Marta, I didn't want to put you on the spot like this. I never would have—"

Marta cut her off. "Of course, you wouldn't. Listen, isn't there anyone else you can call?"

But Rachel knew there wasn't. She would have to make some other arrangement. Perhaps she could stay for a few days at her parents' summer place in Upstate New York. Her mind seized on the idea like a drowning man reaching for a floating log. Yes, that might be the perfect place to retreat for a few days. It would give her a chance to think out her problem in solitude and make some decisions.

Rachel assured Marta she would be okay, mumbled a good-bye, and hung up the phone. She slumped back into the chair, her body limp but her mind racing. For a moment she closed her eyes, tempted to escape into sleep the way she'd done that morning in the hotel. But she knew she couldn't afford the luxury of that. There was too much to get done before tomorrow morning. Though she had told Marta she would be going away for a few days, her plans were much more drastic. Quitting her job as Jason's assistant in such an unprofessional way meant that she was throwing away her teaching position as well. She hadn't thought the whole situation through clearly yet, but perhaps the best thing was to make an entirely clean break. She had some money in the bank, and she could supplement it with tutoring. Even to Rachel the plan sounded unrealistic, but she was in no state of mind to think clearly about the future. It was easier for the moment to concentrate on the small immediate tasks at hand.

First I've got to find the keys to the cottage, she told herself, getting up and beginning to open desk drawers and sift through their contents. *Why can't I be more organized?* she asked herself ruefully, as her fingers closed over and then discarded paper clips, safety pins, and a small stapler. When the keys she sought were finally located, she put them in her purse and then sat down to make a list of the other tasks she would have to complete. There was the packing to be done, the newspaper and mail to be taken care of, the refrigerator to be cleaned out. And of course she would have to notify her landlord. In the back of her mind she knew she was avoiding the real issue by concentrating on trivia. But she was helpless to stop herself.

A loud rap at the door made Rachel's fist clench convulsively around her pencil, snapping the lead off the point. She froze in her chair, eyes riveted to the door. The commanding knock came again, and then the deep voice she knew so well called her name.

"I know you're in there." Jason's tones penetrated the thick wood. "Let me in, Rachel. I don't know what the trouble is, but we've got to get it straightened out."

She didn't move or speak. As though turned to stone, all she could do was stare in horror, hardly breathing. The knock came again several times, and she waited tensely, listening to the frantic thud of her heart against her ribs. The silence in the hall seemed to last forever, but she could sense Jason breathing harshly on the other side of the barrier, his irritation mounting. In her mind's eye she saw his brows drawn together, his blue eyes flash with anger. But the image only served to strengthen her resolve. This was a critical moment, she knew. If she gave in now, she would be lost. Part of her yearned to throw the door open and make everything right between them. She knew that if he drew her into his arms, her mind would stop functioning and her body would begin to rule her brain as it had in Boston. But deep in her heart she knew that things could never really be right between them. And that was why she managed to sit silent and unmoving while Jason paced angrily back and forth, his heels scraping impatiently on the terrazzo floor.

"All right, Rachel, so you're still playing infantile little games," Jason growled. "But I'm not going to let you get away with it. You can stew in your own juice for a while, but I'll be back, and that's a promise."

Rachel held her breath while she listened to the angry sound of Jason's departing footsteps. And then she put her face in her hands as a slow, shuddering breath escaped from her lips. *How can I take any more of this?* she asked herself. *I'm being torn in pieces.* And then Rachel jumped from her chair and went to her room, where she began packing feverishly, throwing clothes frenetically into her suitcase while she made plans. But the burst of artificial energy didn't last long. An hour later she was like an engine sputtering on its last drops of fuel. Exhausted, she fell into bed. Mercifully sleep came soon, and she didn't even hear the repeated ring of the phone in the living room.

But the sun woke her early Sunday morning. For a moment she lay in bed, staring in bleary-eyed confusion at the wavering reflections of light on her bedroom ceiling. Pushing her tangled covers aside and swinging her legs onto the floor, she told herself she might as well get it over with and got up to dress.

Forty-five minutes later she was stuffing her suitcase into the trunk and then heading her car out of the parking lot toward Quincy Adams. As she expected, when she arrived, the liberal arts building was dark and deserted. Thin rays of winter light barely penetrated the gloomy unlighted halls that she traversed to get to the office she and Jason shared. Rachel held her breath for a moment when she got to the door. What if by some mischance he was in there waiting for her? But when she turned the key in the lock and the door swung open, the room was shrouded in darkness. Sighing with a strange mixture of relief and disappointment, Rachel flipped on the light and stepped inside. There were so many memories here, and she wanted her visit to be as brief as possible.

Mindlessly she emptied out her desk drawers, tossing most of what she unearthed into the wastebasket. A few personal items went into her purse. When the task was finally done, she turned uncertainly to Jason's desk, her chest tight and her hands trembling. In all decency she would have to leave him some kind of explanation. But how could she possibly put her feelings into words that made sense? And would Jason even be able to understand her reasoning? Rachel took a deep breath. Maybe not, but she would have to try. Resolutely she opened the middle drawer of his desk in hopes of finding pen and paper.

Pens were scattered across the bottom along with index cards and rubber bands, but file cards wouldn't do for the kind of note she would have to write. Why hadn't she simply taken care of it at home last night? she asked herself. But she knew the answer to that. She had wanted to put this distressing task off till the last possible moment.

The top drawer on the right was more productive. Inside were several unlabeled notebooks. Perhaps she could just tear some clean sheets of paper from them. Pulling out the one on top, she flipped it open and then froze. What she saw was not a blank page. Instead it was filled with Jason's strong, slanted handwriting and bore a disquieting resemblance to the journal entries he had inflicted on her earlier. In fact, as her eyes scanned the page her own name jumped out at her from several lines.

The entry she was examining was dated early October. That would be around the time, she calculated quickly, that he had turned in his first insulting journal to her. Was this something she should be reading? she asked herself guiltily. Obviously he had intended it to be private. But she had gone too far now to look away. Her hands shook as she began to take in the words Jason had penned.

The entry began with a quote Rachel recognized from one of Lord Byron's most romantic poems:

> She walks in beauty, like the night
> Of cloudless climes and starry skies;
> And all that's best of dark and bright
> Meet in her aspect and her eyes.

And who would have thought to have found her teaching Freshman Composition? Why am I afraid to compose my own love poem to Rachel? Is it because I know I can never do her as much justice as a master like Byron? A strange fear, admittedly, for a man who makes his living by the pen. But then with her I desperately want to measure up.

Staggered, Rachel stared down at the words incredulously. Was this some sort of trick? Had Jason really written this? Shaking, she flipped the pages, reading on.

A little farther a paragraph leaped out at her like a lightning bolt:

172

* * *

Coward! Stop hiding behind your sardonic facade.
Let the woman know how you really feel about her.
Or is the great Jason Brand afraid of rejection?

There was more. But Rachel didn't need to read it.
She'd seen enough to turn her whole world around. She
knew now that there was no way she could leave without
finding out for certain what Jason's feelings really were.

Her knees were shaking as she got up from the desk and
put the notebook in its hiding place. *I'll have to go and see
him,* she told herself.

Though she'd never visited him, she knew he was
subletting a luxury apartment in one of the high-rises
bordering Spring Valley, only a few minutes from the
university.

Locking the office behind her, she hurried back to the
faculty parking lot and maneuvered her car out into the
light morning traffic. Her heart was beating fast, and she
was too excited to think clearly. It wasn't until she'd
parked and opened the swinging glass doors to Jason's
building that she glanced at her watch. It was only nine
thirty—early to be dropping in on someone Sunday morning. Would Jason still be asleep? Should she wait? It was
probably the right thing to do. But she knew that she
couldn't. She had to know the answer to her question.

Locating his apartment number on the directory next to
the elevator, Rachel pressed the UP button and waited
nervously for the brushed chrome doors to slide open.
How was she going to approach him? she wondered. She
couldn't very well admit she'd read the journal. Could she
simply come out and ask him about his feelings toward
her?

173

The doors wheezed open, and she stepped inside. Lower lip caught between her teeth, she watched the lights flash hypnotically. When the car bounced to a stop on the tenth floor, she jumped. Once in the carpeted hallway, she looked around uncertainly. Sometimes these buildings had all the odd numbers on one side and the even on the other. All she could do was try left or right at random. But luckily the direction she picked turned out to be correct. Jason's door was at the end of the hall.

However, finding it was one thing and getting up the courage to knock was quite another. Rachel stood for a moment shuffling her feet on the thick oatmeal-colored carpet. What was she going to say to him? Her mind was a blank.

I can't just stand here all morning, she finally told herself impatiently. Raising her hand, she tapped decisively on the painted metal surface. But though she'd made a lot of noise, there was no response from inside. Rachel waited a minute or two, and then, her level of anxiety increasing, she knocked even harder, her knuckles stinging from the impact with the unyielding surface. This time there was an answer. Dimly she heard the sound of slow footsteps and a muttered curse. And then the door swung sharply inward, and Jason stood glowering down at her.

Rachel was shocked. She had never seen him looking this way before. A day's growth of beard shadowed the hard line of his jaw. His hair was tousled into peaks and his eyes were reddened from lack of sleep. Dressed in a faded pair of jeans and a torn sweatshirt, he looked like he might have spent the night in a seedy bus terminal instead of the plushly furnished rooms she glimpsed behind him. But even the rooms showed evidence of disarray. Index cards were scattered about the rug as though they had been flung against a wall, and bottles and glasses littered the coffee table.

"Jason, what's wrong?" Rachel blurted in dismay.

Jason continued to stare at her sardonically. "Well, well, Rachel comes visiting," he rasped, ignoring her question. "Who would have guessed she'd put herself out this way?"

Unprepared for this reception and distressed by his tone, Rachel started to back away. But Jason was having none of that. His mouth tightening grimly, he reached out and seized her by the wrist. Before she could protest, he had dragged her unceremoniously into the room and closed the door behind her with a crash.

"What kind of games are you playing? Why the hell wouldn't you open your door last night?" he snarled, glaring at her with eyes like hard blue stones.

Rachel quailed under the fierce onslaught. "I—I—" she stammered, looking desperately around the room as though it might offer an answer. "Jason, are you drunk?" she finally quavered.

"What the hell do you think? No, I'm not drunk, though it's not for want of trying. I'm too mad to be drunk. I've been pacing the floor all night trying to figure out what goes on in that twisted little mind of yours, Rachel. But so far I've drawn a total blank."

Rachel tried to pull her arm free of his biting grasp. "You're hurting me," she objected with more force than she really felt.

Jason barked a bitter laugh. "Hurting *you*! That's the joke of the century. When it comes to hurting people, you take the prize!"

Rachel eyed him with astonishment. What was he talking about? After reading the tender words in his journal,

175

this was anything but the greeting she had hoped for. It had been a mistake to come here. Her instincts must have been right in the first place. Stung, she clipped out defensively, "I just came to say good-bye. You won't have to worry about me anymore. I'm resigning and leaving town."

Jason's face darkened, and his brows drew together ominously. "You little cheat," he bit out. "Running away is just your style, isn't it? Well, you're not going to get away with it this time. If I have to tie you up to keep you here, we're going to settle this once and for all." Rachel tried to shrink away, but Jason pulled her close to him and then mercilessly frog-marched her to the beige modular sofa.

Pushing her down onto the yielding velvet, Jason stood over her like an inquisitor, his hands planted squarely on his narrow hips.

"Just tell me, Rachel. Why did you let me make love to you in Boston? Did it mean so little to you?"

Determined to retain some shred of dignity, Rachel desperately fought back hot tears. "How can you ask me that?" she whispered, her eyes not meeting the insistent blue of his.

"Because it's damn important that we understand each other for a change, that's why," Jason bit out relentlessly.

How could she tell him just what that magical interlude had meant? Rachel wondered. The words stuck in her throat. The admission would make her even more vulnerable.

"Well . . . ?" Jason persisted.

But Rachel remained stubbornly silent, as though suspended in amber.

Jason made a rough noise in his throat. "Well, then I'll

tell you what it meant to me. I've been in love with you for months, and after that night in Boston I thought you loved me too. But obviously I was mistaken. How could you have given yourself so passionately, Rachel, if it meant nothing? Or were you using me, pretending I was someone else?"

Rachel stared up at him in disbelief, for a moment unable to take in the full meaning of his words. And then a feeling began to flower inside her of such happiness that she felt she might burst.

"Oh, Jason, I love you so much. And I was so afraid that you didn't love me."

She watched while a variety of expressions played across his features. The anger shifted to disbelief and then a spreading delight. She was on her feet then, winding her arms around his neck and clinging to the oaklike solidity of his masculine frame. His own arms returned the embrace, pulling her so tightly against the wall of his chest, she could hardly breathe. Then his lips were against her hair, her cheek, her eyelids—feathering passionate kisses that spoke of his need and desire. And suddenly the sweet flame of Rachel's own desire rose to meet his.

"I want to make love to you," Jason whispered fiercely in her ear. Rachel didn't hesitate, for she was feeling the same urgent want. Tightening her arms around his neck, she molded her body to his hips, communicating the heat that was rushing over her and feeling the burning imprint of his arousal. Gently Jason lowered her to the luxuriantly thick carpet; his questing fingers at the buttons of her blouse opened them so that his lips could nuzzle the softness of her breasts. Her own hands tugged at his sweat shirt. Smiling passionately down at her, he levered his body up to draw it over his head. When the naked skin of

177

his chest was exposed, her fingers reached up to range exploratively over the crisp mat of curling hair. She felt with pleasure the muscular conformation of his chest and the flat hardness of his male nipples. And then her hands slipped boldly to the waistband of his jeans.

"In the way, aren't they?" he chuckled, reaching down to unsnap them and wriggle free. "But so are yours—and your bra too," he added forcefully, unhooking the closure at her back and tossing the wispy garment aside. His head bent to nibble the rosy, hardening tips of her breasts, and then his hand cupped their fullness while his fingers traced erotic circles around them. Trembling with excitement, Rachel felt his hand slip down to the fastening of her own slacks and free it at her waist. And then while his mouth explored the plane of her belly and then sensuously traveled lower to caress her thighs, he slipped one hand underneath the elastic of her lacy panties. Slowly, tantalizingly, his long fingers explored the secret curves and recesses he found there. Involuntarily her breathing quickened as his knowing hand began to weave an erotic pattern of long silken strokes that made her quiver with delicious anticipation. Her fingers twined themselves excitedly in the virile thickness of his hair. And Jason, recognizing the intensity of her response, increased the intimacy of his caress.

"Rachel, love," he whispered, his voice rough with his own passion. But she, lost now in the world of intense sensation he had created, was beyond answering. Her breath was coming in short gasps now, signaling her loss of control. Jason had brought her to a pulsing height from which there was now no return except a complete, trustful surrender to the pleasure he had created for her. Unconsciously Rachel's fingers anchored themselves to Jason's muscular shoulders as she tumbled helplessly off the edge and floated for a timeless moment in the airy, crystal space of her own private ecstasy.

When Rachel returned to reality, she opened her eyes to find Jason looking warmly down into her face. "What have I unleashed?" he questioned, bending to brush his lips against hers. But the kiss that began as a tender endearment changed quickly to heated passion—not just Jason's, but her own as well. As her body arched toward him in rekindled ardor his long arm reached down and slipped her panties from her body.

"Rachel, I want you so much," he groaned. And she felt the truth of his arousal and ached for his complete possession.

The intimate touch of his lips and tongue made Rachel quiver luxuriously. Jason was making her nerve endings pulse with desire, but she wanted to have the same effect on him. Her own hands moved downward, stroking an exploring path across the most sensitive parts of his body. The effect on Jason was galvanizing. Groaning again with ardor, he turned her on her back.

She felt his breath in her ear. "I need you, Rachel. I need you like I need air to breathe. Do you know that?"

"Oh, Jason," she sighed, moving against him in an inborn female response. He entered her with a controlled force that spoke at once of urgency and demand, but also of tender desire.

There was nothing in the world now but the two of them, caught up in an ever-increasing tempo of rapture. Feverishly Rachel's hands clung to Jason's driving hips as he propelled the two of them once more to that high precipice of mutual ecstasy. And the piercing pleasure of it was so overwhelming that she cried out, only to hear his own abandoned cry above her own.

"Oh, Rachel," he whispered, burying his flushed face in her neck. "Never in my wildest fantasies have I dreamed it would be like this."

Nuzzling his hair with her lips and stroking the long line of his naked back with her hand, she murmured her agreement.

Their lovemaking now outshone even the experience in Boston because this time their commitment was complete. Nothing had been held back. And as she lay in Jason's arms, Rachel breathed the heady elixir of total fulfillment.

She felt the touch of his hand lightly brushing the damp hair away from her forehead and looked up to find his blue eyes glittering down at her with warm possessiveness. Then his fingers stroked her reddened cheek where his night's growth of beard had marked her sensitive skin.

"Sorry," he apologized. "I didn't shave this morning because I was so damn worked up about you. And then I just couldn't tear myself away."

Rachel shook her head. "I couldn't tear myself away either. You don't have to take all the blame."

Their gazes locked; the corners of his mouth molded upward in a grin as though he were enjoying some private joke.

Rachel's eyebrows lifted in a question.

"There was something I wanted to give you—something I intended to give you before I threw you on the rug and ravished you. But somehow it didn't work out that way."

Rachel smiled knowingly, the glow from their lovemaking basking over her.

Springing lightly up, he pulled on his jeans while Rachel

watched in puzzlement. Looking down, his eyes took in her nudity with obvious enjoyment. "I like you this way, but I think the occasion calls for a bit more decorum."

Disappearing into an adjoining room, he emerged almost immediately, wearing a white Oxford-cloth shirt in addition to the jeans and carrying a maroon velour robe that he pulled around Rachel's shoulders. Obediently she slipped her arms through the sleeves, which were a good six inches too long. When she had rolled them back and tied the cord, she looked at him questioningly. But he only gestured for her to sit on the couch. When she had done so, he—to her astonishment—went down on one knee and formally presented her with a blue velvet box. Her fingers were trembling as she raised the lid to discover an antique ring, set with a large emerald surrounded by a cluster of tiny diamonds.

"Oh, how beautiful," she breathed.

"It was my grandmother's engagement ring. It's been in my dresser drawer for years. But now it's yours, Rachel, if you want it. That's what I stopped by my father's house for yesterday."

Rachel gazed at him wordlessly.

"Will you marry me?" he asked almost humbly. "I think we can have a good life together, and I can't imagine life without you now."

Strong emotion swept over Rachel. She felt tears pricking the back of her eyes, and she lowered her lashes to conceal them. This was what she had been wanting for so long, but she hadn't really dared to consider the possibility.

"What's wrong?" Jason questioned, moving up to sit beside her on the couch and putting his arm tenderly around her shoulder.

Rachel pressed her palm against his hand. "It's just that I'm overwhelmed. I can't imagine anything more wonderful than being your wife." She hesitated and then plunged on. "But, Jason, do you really want a wife?"

"How can you even ask such a question?" he demanded gruffly. "I've wanted you since that first day you walked into Freshman Comp. It's just that at first I didn't know quite how much I wanted you. I'll admit now that I started off thinking in terms of an affair. But when you started leading me a merry dance, my girl, I realized there was more to it than just physical attraction."

Rachel grinned. "So I was right about you at the beginning!" she teased.

Jason grimaced, "Yes, but you've got to admit that you kept assuming the worst."

"Yes," she conceded in a low voice. "But, Jason, you frightened me. You seemed so tough, so overwhelming. I was already afraid of getting involved with someone who would—who would—" she struggled to explain.

"Who would hurt you again the way Jonathan did?" Jason finished the sentence for her, his mouth tightening with anger. "You don't know how much I hated that bastard for what he'd done. And it was even worse because he was just like my damn father—always after quick gratification to stroke his ego. We get along now, because I understand what makes him tick. But I can't spend much time at home. Watching his escapades is just too upsetting. And then I came to Quincy Adams, and there you were. I didn't know what was wrong with you at first. When I found out you were hung up on the same kind of guy, it damn near tore me apart. Men like that are so good at getting what they want. So you don't know what I went through that night when you turned me down, and then

I found you'd been reading that poem of Convers's. I was so jealous, I couldn't see straight. If he'd been anywhere around, I swear I would have torn him to pieces."

Rachel giggled. "Lucky for the good professor that you didn't get your hands on him. I wouldn't want my future husband behind bars."

Jason gave her shoulder an affectionate squeeze. "Does that mean you'll marry me?"

Rachel's hand flew to her mouth. "Did I forget to say that?"

Jason nodded with mock solemnity. And then, suddenly turning serious, he pulled her into his arms and held her tightly as his lips buried themselves in her hair. "God, I was afraid I was going to lose you," he growled. "I can't tell you how nervous I was when I waited back in the hotel room after you'd left in a huff to go follow Convers."

For a while they held each other in silence, each caught up in the strong emotions of the moment. *What if I hadn't met this man?* Rachel thought, feeling the strength of his arms around her. *What if he hadn't loved me enough to make me realize how foolish I had been?* Finally in a small voice she whispered, "But you were taking such a chance. How could you know I would see Jonathan for what he was?"

"If you hadn't caught on in the lecture hall, I had another plan," he admitted, looking fondly down into her gray eyes. "I was going to get us an invitation to dinner at his house. I knew that if you saw him with his wife and children, that would have ended it for you."

Rachel gave him a startled look that changed quickly to a warm grin. "Jason Brand, you're a dangerous and a devious man. I'm glad you're on my side and not somebody else's."

"I'll always be on your side," Jason said, sealing the pledge with a kiss. "In fact, you know that short story of yours? The one you submitted with your application to Quincy Adams? After my little eavesdropping session in the faculty dining hall, I knew how much your writing means to you. Well, I sent it off to *The Pacific Quarterly* with a note of recommendation describing what a gem of a writer I'd discovered in the ivied halls of Quincy Adams. They've accepted it—and want to see more."

Rachel stared at him incredulously. "You're kidding."

"No."

"But *The Pacific Quarterly* already rejected that story last year. I wanted to get published on my own merit, not because—"

"Darling, it *is* on your own merit. You're a fantastic writer, and they loved the story. The note from me just meant it went to Hal Parsons, the editor in chief, and not some narrow-minded first reader looking for 'formula highbrow fiction.' "

Rachel was stunned. "I don't know what to say. I always dreamed of seeing that story in print, but I'd given up hope."

"Well, there is a way that you can thank me," Jason chuckled.

Rachel pressed her lips quickly to his and then drew back, grinning. "You mean with a big kiss?" she asked innocently.

"I actually had something a bit more demonstrative in mind," he qualified.

"Did you, now," Rachel responded. "Well, first there's one more little detail you need to clear up. Just exactly what is your relationship with your editor—Angelique, I believe her name is."

Jason threw back his head and laughed richly. "Had you worried, didn't I? Well, it was all by design, my dear. Angelique is old enough to be my mother. And that's the role she likes to play with me. I told you I'd been at her house in Connecticut all week. Well, it was true. I couldn't get any work done. All I could do was talk about you and how much I loved you. You know, it was she who finally came up with the idea of taking you off on a research trip. She thought that if I could just get you alone, I could show you what a wonderful catch I was."

"Did she really say that."

Jason raised his hand. "Scout's honor. And now are you finally satisfied?"

Rachel shook her head. "Not yet. But I'm sure you can remedy that situation in the bedroom—after you answer one more little question."

Jason sighed. "Am I never going to get my reward?" he teased.

"Of course. But first tell me why you wrote me those horrible journals."

Jason chuckled. "Shock value, my dear. Simply shock value. And by the way, are you finally admitting that you read my first feeble efforts? Covered with muck in a storm sewer! Really! I thought at the time that you ought to have been able to do better."

Rachel giggled. "Oh, yes, I read it, all right." And then her face reddened. "And I have a terrible confession to make. I read the other journal too—the real journal, I mean. That's what brought me here this morning." She waited fearfully for Jason's reaction. After all, that second journal had been private, something not intended for her eyes.

But instead of anger his response was a sigh of relief.

185

"You know, Rachel, I've been half hoping for a long time that you'd find it. If I really hadn't wanted you to see it, I wouldn't have left it in the desk drawer. It's full of all the things I wanted to say to you. But I was afraid you might laugh."

Rachel shook her head. "I'd never laugh at you," she assured him fervently. "Oh, Jason. I love you so much, and reading that you cared about me, too, made all the difference to me."

Jason grinned wickedly. "Well, if you really love me, I'm afraid you're going to have to prove it—over and over again."

Scooping her up in his arms, he carried her toward the bedroom. "This time we're going to do things properly— in a bed instead of on the living room rug," he whispered in her ear as he strode down the hall.

LOOK FOR NEXT MONTH'S
CANDLELIGHT ECSTASY ROMANCES ®

When You Want A Little More Than Romance—

Try A Candlelight Ecstasy!

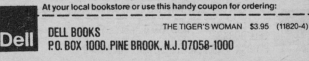

She was a prima ballerina—torn between two men and her passion to dance

Encore

BY MONIQUE RAPHEL HIGH
author of the bestselling *The Four Winds of Heaven*

"A huge, colorful novel. A strong blend of passion, tragedy and art set against the exotic and exciting world of dance." —*Publishers Weekly*

A Dell Book $3.95   12363-1